I0457212

Gold & Poppies

Gar Mac Leman

Dreamcraft Publishing

www.garsong.com/DreamcraftPublishing.html

eBook Published 21st December, 2013

Paperback Published 21st December, 2018

ISBN: 978-0-9924271-1-5

Author's note on the songs

There are three songs, or actually portions of songs, within this manuscript.

1/. Wind Song – written in 1975.
2/. In and Out the Sky – written in 1975.
3/. Unwritten Song – written whilst I was living in Ireland in 1991.

I am in the process of recording all three songs and when they are complete I will include links to them on my own webpage tied in with this book. Check the following link for further details on this book and an update on the recording of the above songs: www.garsong.com/GoldAndPoppies.html

The following links will only become active once the songs are recorded and placed on my website:

www.garsong.com/WindSong.mp3
www.garsong.com/InAndOutTheSky.mp3
www.garsong.com/UnwrittenSong.mp3

1 – Russell

Russell knew the tune the band was playing, sure he couldn't put a name to it, but he did recognise the Irish reel, despite the way the Australian Celtic combo were butchering it. He watched the few girls out on the dance floor jumping around with each other. Probably with the band, he thought as he took a long pull on his pint, drained it, and slipped easily through the half-crowd to the bar.

He shoved in and put the glass down. A tall thin youth with a shaved head and pimple-scarred skin turned and glared at being moved aside. On encountering Russell's even gaze he wandered off. A barmaid appeared and picked up his empty. She was strong faced, almost attractive. Blue eyes beneath close cropped dark hair, which showed some grey despite her being only around twenty five, twenty six.

'Another?'

'Yeh. Guinness.'

The band suddenly changed rhythm and the guitarist began singing his version of the Thin Lizzy classic, *Whisky in the Jar*.

'It's crap isn't it!' The Barmaid put the full pint down.

Russell looked at her and nodded, not smiling, simply agreeing.

'Ahh. You're Irish,' he added, interest materializing as her accent registered. 'I'm a bit slow eh.'

She nodded.

'What's your name then?'

'Una.'

'Not sure of that accent,' he admitted, picking up the pint and taking a deep draught. 'Waterford?'

'Yer not too far out,' she said, smiling. 'Wicklow, but I was livin' in west Cork for a few years before I came over here.'

'County Cork eh. Been there a few times.'

'You got a boyfriend then Una?' he asked, even as he was trying to get himself to turn and walk away.

'I 'aven't and it's not something I'm looking for at the moment.' She held his eyes. 'I had enough trouble with the last one. You trouble then?'

'Not to you.'

'I'll be off at eleven if it stays this quiet.'

'You mean I gotta' listen to this shite for another hour.'

She smiled, shook her head and broke eye contact, turning toward another customer as Russell walked off to a dark corner, as far from the band as he could get.

Una had a flat at the front of an old brick and stone house, in Royal Park. Russell sat opposite her in a faded armchair, they held up their glasses of whisky in a toast.

'Was she Irish too?' asked Una.

Russell looked down and then back up at her. Yeh, he thought, she's perceptive. And yeh, that was attractive, but it also brought on the wariness he constantly tried not to experience with women.

'Is it that obvious?' he asked, knowing he'd already surrendered.

She shook her head and smiled with the corners of thin lips.

'I took a chance and guessed. Reckon you're a hard enough man an' all, but you wouldn't be here if I didn't think you were soft enough, so far as a woman is concerned.'

Russell was on the point of deciding whether to make a move on her or leave within the next few seconds, he'd never know which, for a heavy pounding on the door interrupted. He looked at her in query.

'Ah shit!' she said, obviously with a pretty fair idea of who it was.

'Walk out of here,' she stood and held his gaze. 'Don't get involved. This guy is a nasty arsehole.'

'Don't worry about me,' he smiled, not moving.

'He can be violent,' she insisted, shaking her head, looking decidedly worried. 'He's a biker.'

'Dunno' what makes you think I'm such a nice guy. Let him in.'

Una shook her head again, turned and walked through the kitchen to the front door, which was being assaulted again.

'I told you I didn't want you coming here any more.' Russell heard her slightly raised voice. 'You won't get a second chance to hit me. Get out or I'll call the police.'

'Don't worry about me hitting you,' Russell heard the man say. 'But if you call the police I'll kill you.'

Una came into the room with the biker a couple of paces behind. Russell watched surprise flicker a moment on the bearded face. It transposed to a smile as the big biker anticipated a confrontation. He pushed Una aside and came straight at Russell, probably aiming to get to him still seated.

But Russell was up and grinning as the man arrived. He easily dodged a hastily thrown punch, stepped to the side and hit the biker in the stomach before stepping back and kicking him in the knee.

The biker half fell and quickly struggled back up, breathing heavily, a sharp looking commando knife held in one hand.

He seems to know how to hold it at least. Russell grinned and beckoned the limping man in. The limp vanished as the biker ran toward him, swinging the knife in a wide arc. Russell evaded the pass easily and booted the man in the back as he passed.

The biker turned and began to move in slowly, circling.

'Enough is enough man,' said Russell, still grinning, standing up from his defensive crouch. 'Leave if you don't want to get seriously hurt.'

The biker shook his head, weaving the knife from side to side. Russell shook his head in turn, reached inside his jacket, pulled a gun from its holster and shot his assailant in the leg.

'You're lucky I'm in a good mood,' he said clearly enough that the man clutching his bleeding leg on the floor would get his message. Indeed the biker nodded through the clench of pain. 'Next time we meet **will** be the last.'

Russell watched Una wrap the man's wound tightly, as he'd instructed. He put his mobile away after calling his boss and arranging for a private ambulance to have the man treated where no questions would be asked.

'Will I see you again?' she asked as he opened the door to leave.

'Maybe,' he smiled ironically. He was in two minds about how he felt about Una.

'I see what you meant.'

Russell queried her with a look.

'About not being a nice guy.'

He kept smiling and shook his head yet again.

'So it was an Irish girl tore your heart out?' she asked cryptically.

Russell looked carefully at her face for the first time. A lot of savvy indeed. Blue eyes framed in a network of ever so fine lines. She's been around the block a few times. Time to walk away again?

'Now that'd be telling,' he said, grinning to cover what he felt. As he turned and walked into the night, he was suddenly sure he was lucky it ended the way it did. And he'd taken a little exercise too, jobs had been a bit thin on the ground the last few months. Couldn't afford to get sloppy or complacent. He swam through a maze of memory as he walked toward Port Road. The haze of recollection thicker than usual. He looked for a cab into the city, be a pub open somewhere; leave a few more memories behind.

Though Russell wouldn't, or couldn't, admit where his almost-fear of women came from, with no idea what he could do to correct it, he certainly recognised that of late he was backing out of relationships long before they really got going. If it wasn't a major worry, it was beginning to vex him, and it was always worse when he met someone like Una. Someone he felt he could hook up to without the restrictions and chaos that relationships were so often attached to.

2 — Siao Lin

Siao Lin dragged her gaze from dark storm clouds looming above the ocean. She spun her chair from the window and, standing, selected three pieces of heavily mineralised drill core from the aluminium tray. She wrote out labels, attached them to specimens and slipped the samples into a cotton bag. Hefting it to her shoulder, she brushed a strand of dark hair from her face and walked through to the lab. David, the field assistant, was finishing a run of samples through the absorption photo-spectrometer.

She dropped the bag of rock specimens on the bench to his right.

'I have to run another batch of standards through yet,' he said, looking up. 'But the results seem consistent. They look to be averaging around three percent again.'

Siao Lin nodded. 'If you get time tomorrow, cut me some slides from the samples in that bag.'

'No worries,' David said, as he reached across to grab another test tube.

'Should be done around lunchtime,' he looked up again and smiled. 'Do you want me to run all those new boxes through for copper too?'

'No rush,' she answered. 'But yes, they all need to be done. Box them up and ship them out once they're sampled and analysed.'

David nodded as he slid a thin plastic pipe into another tube of dissolved sample.

Siao Lin asked David if he was coming to dinner, but he said no, he'd rather get the work finished. Good to have someone so keen on their job, she thought as she turned and walked out into the pale green corridor. Seeing the light on in Peter's office, she tapped at the door, paused a moment, and entered.

'Oh hi Sue,' said Peter, looking up. 'I was hoping to catch you this evening.'

Siao Lin smiled faintly at his shortening of her name. She wondered how such an informal man ever got a chief geologist's position, let alone kept it. He looked like an oversized boy despite obvious years of hard living. He must sleep in his suit, she thought, looking at the creased and crumpled fabric, and that hair…

'I was just going to have some dinner,' she said. 'Care to join me?'

The smell of his aromatic pipe tobacco registered on her senses. Tobacco smoke was one of her pet hates, reminding her of the pollution in Shanghai she'd endured to obtain her degree. She drew a deeper breath and realised the smell was actually quite pleasant.

'No time girl,' he said, gesturing briefly with upturned hands. 'I'll have to fly out tonight after the storm. How is the sampling on the new hole?

She smiled, reached into her pocket and extracted a piece of drill core.

'We're out through the edge of the granite again,' she said, passing him the specimen. I can see fine flakes of molybdenite as well as galena.'

Peter looked at the sample.

'Hmmm. Could well be.' He nodded and studied the specimen. 'Get Dave to send enough crushed sample off to check for both lead and molybdenum. Do the entire hole.'

Peter asked her about the copper percentages and was happy enough with three percent. He asked her to do a final report on the latest drill-holes and provide recommendations for any extra holes she thought might be needed.

To get back to her room, Siao Lin took the long way, around the outer gantry, where she could look straight down to the shaded sea beneath. She loved to watch the large fish swimming between the huge legs which supported the drilling platform. As a child she'd fished with Uncle Yuan many times. Well, he'd fished, she'd always cleaned the catch. It wasn't just because I was a woman, she thought. Uncle Yuan broke with tradition and taught me the old ways of Gung Fu, which had been passed down in our family since the Shaolin temples were destroyed. She smiled as she watched a giant trevally cruising amongst schools of smaller fish.

Thunder from the approaching storm rumbled louder. Siao Lin looked up to see the clouds sweeping in; the storm was closing.

In her room she showered and changed clothes, glad as always to get out of the old sweaty ones. The cafeteria wasn't far, walking along the corridor she heard rain and hail begin to lash the roof.

She ate by a window, watching the storm's fury as night enclosed the platform. Blinding flashes of lightning showed glimpses of a low, roiling cloudbase; such tropical ferocity was something one got used to quickly in equatorial regions.

Thoughts drifted back to the previous year; to her blatant bribery of Chinese Communist Party officials. Half the remaining gold, sent out by her great grandfather, had been used in getting her permissions and visas. It had been her own hard work studying, which had led to her obtaining the position of research geologist for Exminoil, a position which perfectly suited her major in petrology. The two months she'd spent on the rig so far had been interesting, if a trifle frustrating. Siao Lin felt her real goal was to check out the area, in Australia, where her great Grandfather had vanished back in the mid-1800s. Part of her felt life would not really begin until she got to Australia and made an effort to visit where Tamo had actually been. She would try to trace his journeys, even though she realised her life was going quite well, and such thoughts were partly fantasy, it was one of her childhood ambitions. Searching for copper on Manos Island was a bit on the boring side too, still she was patient and could indeed feel the world opening up for her.

Siao Lin's thoughts were interrupted by some boisterous activity at the bar of the cafeteria. Several drillers and offsiders were drinking quickly and talking too loudly. A minute later, one of the younger men approached her table and asked drunkenly if she would join them. She declined politely, citing further work, and right away decided to leave unobtrusively as soon as she could manage.

Siao Lin laughed inwardly at the antics of the drillers. Her thoughts again flew to finally getting to Australia. One more month of work and the company would fly her anywhere she wanted for two weeks, and it would be Australia she'd visit, without a doubt.

The yelling of the drunken men interrupted her thoughts again and she slipped out quietly when they were engaged in a bout of arm wrestling and appeared to be paying no attention to her.

She walked the long way around the outer scaffolding again, hearing the choppy sea releasing the storm's energy on the supporting pylons below. The rain had passed, thunder continued to rumble in the distance; she could sense the ozone and felt enervated, not the least slowed by having just eaten. She leaned on the safety railing and gazed down at the choppy water far below. She noticed the flash of a long silver fish as it darted from a shaded pylon and vanished into the depths, and idly wondered what sort of fish it had been.

She heard a scuffle behind. Instinctively she turned, already realising her escape from the canteen had not gone unnoticed.

Three of the men from the bar closed in. Siao Lin, immediately sensing the precarious nature of the situation tried to move off, but a large, heavy man with a shaven head blocked her way.

'You must be lonely out here,' he leered, as he looked her up and down. 'I've got something that'll make sure you're satisfied.'

Siao Lin stepped back a pace, he was a big strong man, and she already knew no good would come from the confrontation. The smell of sweat and a stale odour of alcohol drifted from him. His slurred speech and unsteady gait showed how drunk he was. Surely she could slip past him easily. She feinted left and then moved right. But she had moved far too quickly, he hadn't time to react to her feint, simply stood still, blocking her way. He reached forward to try and grapple her.

'Leave me alone,' she said, stepping back, aware she was close to the two behind. 'I'll call security.'

The other two suddenly grasped her arms from either side. The third laughed as he approached.

'Was that a threat?' The big man laughed as he moved toward her.

Siao Lin prepared herself mentally for what she now knew was inescapable.

'I am a Buddhist,' she said clearly and evenly, twisting somewhat to test the grip on her arms. It was strong and tightened further as she struggled.

'I refuse your offer of aggression and violence and warn you that whatever actions you take toward me will be returned to you.'

Drunken laughter followed her words, time to act.

Using the holds applied to her arms as a fulcrum she kicked hard at the man approaching. The added leverage surprised her. She felt her right foot strike its intended target hard. Too hard, I kicked him far too hard.

She used gravity and the rebound from the kick to regain her feet momentarily, acting so quickly there was little time to think. The men holding her tightened their grips. They smelled bad. Their fingers dug painfully into her arms. The man she'd kicked was unconscious and collapsing to the cold hard decking, she hoped briefly she hadn't killed him.

'Throw her over the edge,' muttered the man holding her left arm, pushing her toward the safety mesh. She felt the man on her right side loosen his grip as he moved to follow the other's lead.

Siao Lin bent her knees slightly and pressed hard with her toes, back somersaulting, using their grips as anchor points. Her right arm slipped free, and as she compensated, she felt the other man loosen his grip too. Her arm slipped through his grasp. As her feet contacted the grating again, she leaned right to absorb momentum. She turned her body leftward, using the turn to aid the strike of her right arm, hitting the man on her left with the heel of her right palm. She felt a bone in his jaw break as pain from the blow jarred her own nervous system.

My hand is broken. Somehow her thinking remained cold and almost unaffected by the agony. Neither adrenaline nor pain dented her composure, thanks to childhood training. The man dropped to the floor, semi-conscious, moaning. Siao Lin turned to face the third attacker. He had produced a stubby knife, and was waving it toward her.

'I won't accept your violence,' she repeated, trying to keep the agony she felt in her wrist and hand from affecting her dialogue.

The young man feinted quickly to the left and then the right. Siao Lin didn't move, but stayed crouched forward, waiting. She realised she might need to use her broken hand. As soon as he began his lunge forward, she knew she'd be alright. He ran forward and thrust the knife at her stomach, appearing to have no real knowledge of knife fighting. Both her arms moved to the left automatically, her right arm lifting his lunging hand to her left, clear of her body. As soon as the attack was safely averted her left arm snapped down as the right continued up.

The crack of the young man's forearm was clearly audible and followed by a scream of agony. His knife clattered on the metal gridding as he crouched into a slump. Siao Lin, still in motion, brought her left elbow back and struck the side of his face. He collapsed, unconscious.

Siao Lin drew a deep breath and held it, pushing against the agony, motionless, save for a slight trembling. The distant throb of a diesel generator and the slapping of the waves far below were the only sounds above her racing heartbeat. She looked down at the three unconscious men. She lifted her wrist and could see white bone, broken, visible through translucent skin. Shaking her head in disbelief she turned and walked back the way she'd come, toward the canteen.

She managed the door from the outer scaffolding, and a uniformed security guard pushed out through the swinging doors of the canteen, immediately spotting her. He ran the few metres to her side.

'Are you alright Siao Lin?' he asked as he reached her.

She recognised Chris. 'My hand is broken.'

She paused to draw a deep breath against the continuing waves of pain.

Chris used his phone and called for the medic.

'There are three badly injured men back on the gantry,' said Siao Lin shakily, tense with pain.

Despite her pain, worry resurfaced. The first man she'd kicked had dropped like a stone. She took another deep breath and held it, pushing against the agony. Chris walked her inside the cafeteria and sat her down. She tried to relax, hurting but knowing she was safe. Someone lifted her arm. Siao Lin looked up and recognised the medic, closed her eyes, dropped her head again. She heard talking and felt the prick of a needle before thoughts became dreams and swirled her off, back to China and her youth.

3 — Discord

The room was a world of contrasts. Dirty dishes, each with its own selection of cutlery, littered the sink. Most nearby cupboards were open and closing in on empty. A writing desk, home to both a desktop computer and a laptop, was clean and well-ordered, yet the rubbish bin beside the desk, overflowed with rolled up paper. Half a metre depth of assorted dirty clothing adorned a bedside chair, yet several well dusted photographs ornamented a bureau which contained a collection of antique bottles. A table by a sofa, whose chair was aimed at a tiny television set, was littered with beer cans of the XXXX variety, and several empty bottles of Jamieson's Black Label.

Russell lay across the bed, tangled in clean sheets, a thin blanket crumpled on the floor nearby. His steady snoring was punctuated by the ring tone of his mobile. On hearing the phone, he sat up and stretched for it, still untangling sheets as he spoke.

'Russell,'

'Yeh, Ok Dave,' he said evenly after a few seconds. 'Be there in ten.'

'I believe you Russell,' said Dave, seated behind his desk. 'Look, I'll put in a brief to show the events as you've related them.'

'He was lying though!' exploded Russell. 'I wasn't drunk. I shot the man in self-defence, simply thought it best to keep it quiet…'

'Okay Russell,' Dave cut him off. 'It was a bad thing. Shit happens, I don't want to go there. But! Simple fact. You gotta' get over it, especially if you want to keep working here. Don't give Bill any more reasons.'

'He wouldn't be here if he wasn't your brother in law Dave,' said Russell.

'Yeh I know,' said Dave, holding up both hands, palms toward Russell.

'Just try and avoid getting into those situations, and, you got to dry out man.'

'Dave, you know me better than that.' Russell said evenly. 'I've never drunk on duty, never will. Bill's been shitty with me since I saved his arse. He used to be half way decent, reckon he's just about lost it.'

'I'm watching him too Russell, and they're watching me. Just do me a favour and lay low for a while.'

'I could use some work Dave.'

'Yeh I know Russ, I'm happy enough it's quite though. God knows, we don't need any terrorist attacks or national security issues really, do we.'

Russell turned on hearing the door open. Bill walked in between the two security guards. Russell stared at him with evident malice.

Bill was tall and lean, with scraggly thinning hair. His clothes seemed a couple of sizes too big. He nodded to Dave, ignoring the steady look Russel maintained, and walked to his desk. He dropped a folder down, extracted and stowed a few papers, and stapled several sheets together. He hit the on switch of his computer, and shuffled a few more sheets of paper around before walking over to stand a metre in front of Russell.

'You were pretty drunk Russell,' he said. 'I could hear it in your voice.'

'And I could hear you were an arsehole Bill,' said Russell evenly. 'Didn't mean I needed to tell everyone.'

'I was just doing my job…'

'Tell you what Bill,' said Russell, cutting him off and stepping closer, right into his face. Their eyes were of a height.

'I still want to work here, so I'll leave you alone. If I decide to quit I just may kill you first. At very least I'll beat the crap outa' you.'

'Fuck you too Russell.' Bill wasn't going to back down.

Russell held his position for a few seconds before turning, winking at Dave, who was frowning at the sudden turn of events, and walking to the door.

'Catch you Dave,' Russell called over his shoulder.

'I'm not scared of him Dave,' said Bill, turning to face Dave, across his desk, as the door slid closed behind Russell.

'You should be,' said Dave, sitting back down and leaning back in his chair. 'Just leave him alone Bill, I won't tell you again.'

For a few seconds Bill looked as if he would continue the talk, but thought better of it and walked back to his desk.

4 – Coffs Harbour

One moment she was a five year old, scurrying along the bank of a mud-yellow river in southern China, shortly before sunrise. Pale light began to seep through closed eyelids.

Closed eyes? The dream washed aside; the scurrying of thoughts intruded. Siao Lin marvelled at the soft green light. Her eyes flickered open and then shut involuntarily, squeezed tight as the room's brightness overwhelmed. Thoughts arose. The 'what happened?' was partially resolved with memories of the attack. And her injury, yet she felt no pain? Where am I, re-opened her eyes. Squinting, she moved her head faintly on neck muscles, tight and painful from disuse.

'Good to see you awake girl.'

She adjusted her focus and found Peter sitting in a chair on the dimmer side of the room.

'Where am I?' She asked, already more relaxed for his presence.

'You're in the Coffs Harbour Base Hospital and your wrist operation is finished, clean breaks, easily repaired.'

Siao Lin lifted her right arm, which lay outside the covers. A thick white wad of plaster covered her arm from elbow to fingertips.

'The men who attacked me?'

'One of the men died Siao Lin.' Peter came straight out with it.

She nodded as her worry about the incident solidified into reality.

'I'd been worried about him,' she half-mumbled. 'The other two were holding me, it was hard to judge.'

'It must be hard…' began Peter.

'I could have acted no other way.' She spoke before he could continue. 'I did warn them. Will there be repercussions?'

'No. The incident occurred between Papuan and international waters. You're in Australia now and there are no ramifications. Exminoil will stand by you in full. Somewhere down the line you'll need to decide if you want to take action against the men who attacked you.'

'I can tell you that now,' she said, having thought about it immediately after their assault. 'I have no need for retribution.'

Peter nodded. 'We can have you out of here in a few days. Be at least a month before you have to decide what you want to do. Coffs Harbour is a nice town. You can live it up on company expense.'

The medicinal smell of the hospital seemed to bore down on Siao Lin as she looked about. The air was still, heavy and stuffy. There was no pain, but she felt tired and sleepy still, despite having just woken.

'I'd like to get out of here as soon as I can,' she said as Peter stood, an obvious precursor to his leaving.

Peter nodded. 'I can understand that. I'll see if we can get you out in the morning tomorrow. How about a nice resort, in fact I'll go and arrange it now. Catch you later.'

'Okay,' nodded Siao Lin as Peter left. She closed her eyes and drifted in chaotic thoughts awhile, before slipping asleep.

'How do you feel?' asked the Chief Geologist as they walked across the hospital carpark.

'I'll be alright,' she said, seeing no need to voice further concerns.

Looking about, she could see mountains close by. The sky was clear and bright blue, and the air was warmish, despite the early hour. I'm in Australia at last, she thought, elated as she suddenly realised a large part of the goal she had set herself so many years before, had become a reality.

'I've booked you into the Park Beach Motel Resort,' said Peter as he opened the door of a small car.

Siao Lin climbed in.

'It's right on the beach, you'll love it. We'll call into the bank on the way through town. I've opened an account for you. Exminoil owes you quite a bit in wages but you'll be operating on this expense credit card for the time being.'

He handed her a visa card which she studied as Peter started the car and drove off.

Over the next few days, Siao Lin found the Motel to be everything Peter had claimed. The food was good, the beach lovely and she could walk, or catch a cab into the shopping district and relax in the cafes and coffee shops. The only dislike she had, and it was a minor one at first, was that the place was so busy, so full of people. Many of them seemed ostentatious and loud. She didn't actually feel intimidated, but would simply have preferred somewhere quieter and less hectic.

The third day after leaving the hospital, Siao Lin spent several early morning hours walking around Mutton Bird Island. She watched some young boys fishing off rocks, often having to jump back as choppy waves splashed and broke about them. They showed her the bream they'd caught, which looked similar to fish she'd caught in China.

She walked back along the breakwater, marvelling at the variety of boats moored in the large marina. She ate fresh fish at the small seafood restaurant nearby. To her geologist's sight, the rocks of the island had been boring, lacking mineralisation, but the walk back along the foreshore was memorable. At one point she even removed her shoes and rolled her shorts higher to wade across the mouth of a small river.

Siao Lin leaned her left hand on her door to fit the key. The door opened unexpectedly as soon as she touched it. The lock was torn off on the inside. As she entered, the disarray of her room was shocking. Someone had been through everything hurriedly.

She soon discovered how efficient the burglar had been. Her passport and credit cards were gone, as was the little cash she'd had. Far worse was the loss of two gold nuggets, each about an ounce in weight, which had been concealed in a small bronze statue of a dragon. The gold had been sent back to China from Australia, by one of her ancestors, Tamo, in the mid-1800s.

The resort had seemed so relaxed and secure. Siao Lin felt tears on her cheeks. She shook her head to refute them, tried to lock the door, but gave up and walked to the manager's office.

'Similar thing happened a month ago,' agreed Graham, the Assistant Manager, shaking his head in dismay after she'd told him what had happened. 'Don't know what this area is coming to. Use my phone to call your bank right away and let them know. I'll arrange a cab to take you in to them. We'll cover any damages you suffered of course.'

You can't cover the things I really didn't want to lose, she thought, shaking her own head slowly in turn. The loss of the two pieces of gold weighed heavily on her mind; losing them to a thief, after they'd travelled so far, over such a length of time, felt like a tragedy.

Peter will be in New Guinea, she thought, as Graham again asked her what she wanted to do. I'll have to do what I can myself.

'Call me a taxi right away,' she said evenly, almost choking on the words and coughing to cover her distress.

'I will go straight to the bank. My passport was stolen too, will I be alright to travel without it.'

'That won't be a problem,' said Graham, as he stepped to his desk and picked up the phone. From his demeanour, she got the distinct impression that he just wanted her out of the place, but she said nothing further. It was what she wanted too.

5 — Sawtell

Siao Lin had difficulty at the bank. Even after they phoned and confirmed with the resort that her ID had been stolen, they only agreed to cancel her cards. She left feeling unhappy and disillusioned, for the first time wondering how tenuous her stay in the country was.

As they turned onto the highway, she asked the taxi driver if he knew a place she could move to. Sleeping in the room which had been burgled didn't appeal to her at all.

The driver, Barry, seemed enthusiastic, and agreed to take her to the Boambee Resort, at Sawtell, a town almost a suburb Coffs Harbour. A friend of his ran it and the security was very good. On the way there he drove her up to a lookout, turned the engine off and they both got out.

'Over there is where you'll be staying,' said Barry, pointing down to a heavily treed area, nestled in the curve of a deep river. 'Thought I'd give you a view of the area first.'

She could clearly see a railway bridge and a thin line of sandy beach. Thick trees and bushes occupied a low area, the faintest pale outlines of buildings showed through the screening trees.

'The town is about half a mile further on to the south,' he added, pointing to where a series of sandy beaches and headlands stretched away to the south, the more distant washed out with haze from the breakers. The town was partially hidden by a scrubby hills covered with isolated houses and trees.

Two hours later, Siao Lin watched the taxi drive away, locked her room and walked down to the water's edge. She was intrigued by several fish she noticed swimming about and further amazed by two dolphins which she watched moving up the river. Tim, the manager, found her walking back to her room and informed her that the Park Beach Motel had called him. They would cover her bill for the time being, forwarding the costs to Exminoil.

She immediately fell in love with the small seaside town. The rocky headland and the long sandy stretch of beach with its crashing breakers were intriguing. She enjoyed a snack and coffee at the Sawtell Surf Life Saving Club often, sitting under faded umbrellas, where the view of the beach, from chrome chairs and tables, was pleasant. She visited the Chinese restaurant every few nights. The owner was from Hunan province in China, and had a good knowledge of the Szechuan style of cooking, which Siao Lin preferred. He often joined her after the meal and she enjoyed speaking in a language more familiar than English.

Peter turned up a week later with a new credit card. He told her over a delightful dinner in the small restaurant at the resort how the two driller's offsiders had been sacked immediately and flown back to Australia from the Pt. Moresby hospital. He asked her to think about what she wanted to do. Did she want to return to New Guinea, or take up a position elsewhere within the company? They had projects all over the world. He went on to suggest a third option.

Due to the nature of the ordeal she'd been through, Exminoil would pay out her contract. They would continue to cover her expenses until her injuries were healed and then relocate her anywhere she desired.

Siao Lin remained quiet while Peter voiced the options available. His last suggestion seemed very generous. Why would they offer so much. Her contract was for two years, and if paid in full, she would have a substantial sum, more than a lifetime's wage for many back in China.

Peter began talking about how nice a place she seemed to have picked to stay in and on the quality of the chicken tandoori he was eating.

'If I accept a payout,' asked Siao Lin. 'Can I remain in the country?'

Peter looked at her, smiling somewhat as he chewed and swallowed the mouthful he was eating.

'You want an Australian passport you mean?' he asked, almost grinning.

'I telephoned the Chinese Embassy to renew my Chinese passport, but that will take some time and probably require me to bribe someone.'

'I think we can do it alright,' he looked thoughtful. 'Hard to say for sure. It'll have to be done while you're still employed by

Exminoil. You'd want a driver's licence too I suppose.'

Siao Lin nodded again, and smiled. Free of obligations, she would finally be able to try and track down what happened to her ancestor.

Peter promised to do what he could to help her get an Australian passport, adding it would take a few weeks. He left as soon as the meal was finished and Siao Lin went back to her room, feeling excited and not at all like going to bed. Luckily the long day caught up with her and she fell asleep as she was reading and didn't wake until the sun was bright on the curtains of her room.

The restful sleep, along with what Peter had said the night before had taken the edge off the disharmony Siao Lin had been feeling of late. She resolved to take things as they came, walking along the seashore for an hour or so before a light breakfast. So pristine was the coastline, she couldn't help but think about the conditions in China, particularly in Shanghai, where the pollution was horrific. She realised how lucky the people living in this area were and doubted they realised it all.

6 – Thieves & Gold

Russell Gibb was sitting at a roulette table in the casino at the Adelaide Railway Station. He was up two grand and absently wondering when they'd stop him using the simple system he was employing. He was betting black and doubling his bet each time he lost, returning to the original ten dollars once he'd won. He knew a few of the security guards and thought they'd step in soon. Not that he cared; he wasn't even sure why he bothered. It wasn't the money, he had what he needed.

He looked at the clock on the far wall. Eight fifteen. He'd been there since three am. Nearly time for breakfast, especially now the alcohol had worn off. He lifted his chips and headed to cash in. One of the security men nodded to him and smiled, been about to bar him more than likely. They'd tolerate systems for a little while but best not to push too far or make a habit of it.

Those birds are too bloody loud he thought as he walked out onto the street and took a deep breath of exhaust fumes. Country might be nice for a while.

He felt his phone buzzing before he heard it. First time it'd rung in three weeks. Oughtn't to be more about that biker he shot, that'd been sorted with Dave. Bloody Bill. Need to hammer him into line one of these days. He took the phone out and despite being certain who was calling, checked the number of the incoming call.

'Russell,' he said slowly, in a deep voice indicating neither the irritation at being interrupted doing nothing, nor the tinge of excitement, wondering about the upcoming job, if it was one.

The reply to his greeting was brief in the extreme.

'ASAP,' he replied.

Sounded like a job alright. He quickly turned to one of the waiting cabs rather than walk the kilometre through city streets. Streets were busy enough too, looked like mostly workers headed to jobs, every one walking fast. The cab threaded through the traffic quickly, making for the square and the old *Central Market*. He got out on the far side and watched in shop windows as he walked around the block. He had no tail, and anyway, why would he?

Russell casually entered an electrical goods store, just off the market proper and wandered about, apparently appraising the stock on display. No one entered the shop behind him and at a nod from one of the salesmen, he walked out through the back and punched in his combination at a heavy security door.

The door opened and he was greeted by a tall thin man, who simply nodded a greeting as he passed. Through a room of cameras, past two further security guards and an automatically opening door, where his boss Dave, a heavyset, balding man, sat smiling up at him.

'Come in Russ,' he said, standing and stepping out from behind the desk to shake hands.

Russell nodded a greeting as they shook hands, and sat in the proffered chair as Dave also sat down behind his desk again.

'Reckon you'll be happy enough to have something to do at last,' he said.

'Was I complaining?' he replied, returning the smile; the standard joke. 'What have you got anyway?'

Doesn't seem like a big deal Russ,' said Dave, handing a plastic folder across. 'Have a quick read, got you booked on a flight in an hour and a half.'

Russell skipped through the pages. Some gold had turned up. It came from an unknown source and was high in cobalt, very high in cobalt. It piqued the interest of some high level characters in the U S of A and they asked us to track down where it came from.'

'Still workin' here are you?'

Russell looked up to see Bill Calaglio glaring down at him.

'Jesus Bill, you scared the crap outa me,' he laughed at the comical figure looming over him. 'You look like a worn out scarecrow.'

'Fuck you too!' said Bill turning and striding away.

'You read that stuff Russ?' asked Dave, reaching forward and tapping the folder on the desk.

'I've a general idea,' he replied. 'I'll get into more detail on the plane.'

'Give us a call if you need anything then,' said Dave. 'I know I said this wasn't much, but there are some big players interested.'

Russell nodded, scooped up the folder and stood. Dave nodded as Russell raised his hand in farewell and turned to leave the office.

By the time Russell walked off the airbus in Melbourne, he'd read about the pieces of gold and partially understood the way tellurides were analysed to provide an accurate source location for a sample. So far the only connection they had with the nuggets in question was with a man named Neville Horne, who was mining tailings for gold in a town named Edgerville, near Ballarat.

He walked through the milling travellers and collected keys to a Toyota Hi-lux from a hire company as arranged by his organisation. An hour and a bit later he turned off the highway at a town named Garden and travelled a further five kilometres to the small gold mining town of Edgerville.

Thick old pine trees partially lined the roadway, shadowing and obscuring his vision as he reduced his speed per the signage. Mine workings were visible off to the left and across a couple of scruffy weed-filled fields were 2 dams. Beyond was what was left of the Government Battery he had seen marked on his map. Neville Horne was mining acreage just beyond, sifting through unmined overburden and old mine dump material and leaching it for gold. He had been finding barely enough to finance his efforts and it was the sudden appearance of two nuggets, quite out of character, which had sparked official interest.

Russell turned left onto a coarsely gravelled road, hearing the loud bark of a heavily built Labrador which ran along, just inside a wire fence, paralleling the track. He followed the track around to the left, and pulled over to park at a half closed gate. The area was heavily fenced. He walked through the mangled gate, with the white painted Government Battery on his left. He could literally see the reclamation of old tailings taking place. A large front end loader was scraping the yellow red surface layers of clay and gravel and depositing it into a wedge shaped bin. Cyanide treatment would extract what gold had been missed in the days of the goldrush boom. He jumped up through a cloud of thick dust, onto the earthmover and shouted to the driver, who spotted him quickly and leaned forward him in an effort to hear.

'Where's the boss?' he asked.

The man pointed to a ramshackle caravan a hundred metres or so further into the property.

'Ees probably still sleepin' in there mate,' he yelled, blue eyes bright and framed by dusty crow's feet.

Russell nodded his thanks and sprang easily down, allowing the huge machine to turn and recommence its dusty task. He walked toward the caravan, eyes scanning for any sign of movement. The mobile home had probably been silver in its youth, but dents and scars combined with rust and several colours of paint, to emphasise what it'd been through over the years. It was poorly supported and lay askew, propped up by empty oil drums and several large boulders of quartz.

He checked to the rear, but rolls of fencing wire and rusty stakes blocked the way. Without a knock, he unclipped the narrow metal door and stepped in. He could see a hunched figure, beneath the sprawl of untidy blankets at the low end of the van. The man may have been hung over, but he was alert enough and Russell noticed immediately that he was a big man, looking quite strong indeed.

'Who're you?' The miner sat up, dislodging most of the bedcovers, revealing his fully clothed status. 'Didn't hear you knock.'

'I didn't,' said Russell, stepping forward quickly and pushing the man back down onto the bed. 'I've got a few questions for you. Just stay down there and answer me.'

'You the law then?'

'Is your name Neville Horne?' asked Russell slowly.

Neville nodded, propping himself onto his elbows.

'You sold two large nuggets a few weeks ago,' said Russell, slowly and evenly. 'Where did you get them?'

'I got them here,' said Neville, gesturing out the window, trying to sit up further.

Russell pulled his fingertips back, away from his palm as he directed his hand toward the underside of the man's jaw. He stepped back sharply as the miner slumped backward, stunned by the blow. His hands reached for his jaw and Russell could see him moving his chin as he grimaced.

'Next time I will break it,' he said calmly, holding Neville's gaze with his blue eyes. 'Answer the question.'

'I can't,' stammered Neville. 'You don't mess with people like them.'

'You don't mess with me Nev',' said Russell, slowly and evenly. 'I'm not giving you a choice. Answer now and avoid further pain. You can keep the money for the gold, we just want to find out where it came from.'

'Dominick Wright,' spat the miner, looking down. 'He has a second-hand goods, pawn shop in Coffs Harbour.'

'Shop's a front then?' asked Russell.

'Maybe,' said Neville. 'Reckon so,' he added quickly. 'Reckon he might have connections.'

'If it makes you happier Mr Horne,' said Russell as he edged backward. 'He won't find out where I got his name at all, so if I were you I'd simply deny it.'

Russell left the door and walked evenly across the dusty mining area. The two machines were continuing their work as he passed them. He lifted his hand in greeting to the driver he'd spoken to earlier. He sat in his Toyota, called Dave and asked for as much info as they had on Dominick Wright to be emailed for access once he'd arrived at Coffs Harbour.

7 — Betrayed

For four weeks Siao Lin walked along beaches and trails through rain forested hills. Most days she enjoyed a coffee and light lunch at the Sawtell Surf Lifesaving club, overlooking the ocean.

Peter phoned after a week and said Exminoil had agreed in principal to her request, although they said they'd be sorry to see her go.

Barry took her to the hospital after four weeks. They removed her cast and x-rayed her hand again. The doctor was happy with her progress and said the cast could stay off, but she would need to be careful for a while. The wrist looked so pale and weak, but she knew time and exercise would soon strengthen it. He suggested bandaging the wrist and forearm regularly, but agreed Siao Lin could swim a little.

She only watched the swimmers at the surf beach, where the ferocity of the waves was scary. She'd never experienced surf before and just paddled about in the shallows during the afternoon heat. She watched the children, easily catching the waves and riding them into the shore. She would try it one day, but not until her wrist was fully healed. She did swim a little some evenings, stroking slowly out into the current off the beach at the river near the resort. Swimming a little every day soon had her feeling better, but she was still shy of the thundering surf of the main beach.

A week after she had her plaster off, Peter turned up again. He drove her through Coffs Harbour, to a resort further north where they ate. After they'd ordered their meal, he opened his small brief case and extracted a thick envelope.

'Everything you want is in here,' he said, smiling as he passed it across.

Despite her eagerness to investigate, she decided to play it cool.

'Thanks for everything Peter,' she said, placing the still sealed envelope beside her plate. 'I don't know how to thank you.'

'You can come back and work for me Sue,' he said.

Is he joking, she thought?

'Aren't you going to look in there,' he said still smiling.

She picked up the envelope and opened it. Everything she'd asked for was inside, a new Australian passport, a NSW driver's licence, several bank cards along with paperwork confirming the payout she'd received from Exminoil.

Peter informed her that officially she would still be in the employ of Exminoil, the job being a necessity when applying for her Australian passport. He asked her if she had any idea where she'd go or what she wanted to do. She wasn't wholly truthful to him, saying she had no idea, even though she knew she'd head off pretty soon and try to trace the travels of her ancestor.

'How's your hand?' He asked, looking at the bandage.

'It's pretty good now,' she said, holding it up between them and flexing fingers.

'When I first had the plaster off it was a bit tight, but the swimming has helped a lot.'

The waiter arrived with their entrees and their discussion ceased.

Two hours later, Peter dropped her home and walked her to her room. She waved goodbye and walked inside, kicked off her shoes and sat down.

30 seconds after she'd sat down Siao Lin decided to walk to the beach and enjoy the pleasant night. She put on soft shoes and slipped out the door, Peter's car was already gone. Turning left, she followed the narrow walking trail which led toward where the pointed headland poked out into the estuary. Walking in near complete darkness presented no issue, and she turned off, along a narrow tree-lined trail toward the start of the sandy beach.

As she emerged from the shrubs and onto the sand she heard a voice. A car was silhouetted against the distant street lights on the hill above. She thought it was Peter's car and so walked across the sand toward it. The air was faintly warm, an ideal temperature, and she could feel the cool of the sand as it touched her feet above the low shoes. A small wave dumped on the beach; the distant crump and slap turned her head and she stopped walking.

She turned back. It was Peter. She could see his face silhouetted by a light on the main road above. She could hear his voice, she should call him… Was about to when his words reached her through the still night air.

'I can't just ask her where the gold came from.' Peter had raised his voice. 'How can I explain our interest without her thinking we were involved in the theft?'

He paused for a few seconds. Siao Lin stood motionless, part of the night's darkness behind her. She shivered with a chill, despite it not being cold.

'I know we weren't involved, but it'll look like that to her,' he sounded almost apologetic. 'You'll just have to keep someone on her for a while and see what eventuates. If you'll give me the gold back, I could give it to her and then ask. Now that would be reasonable.'

He paused for a longer time.

'My hands are tied then,' he said, sounding stressed.

Siao Lin had lost whatever prohibition she'd had about eavesdropping; she lowered herself to the faintly warm sand, unbelieving.

'No, I told you before. It can't have come from anywhere she's been since she's been working with us.' He sounded animated and upset.

As Peter paused and shook his head, obviously listening and disagreeing, Siao Lin had heard enough. She stood and moved silently back across the sand and into the trees. As she reached her room, she heard a distant car door slam and then an engine start. A car drove off.

She walked inside, leaving the light off, her heart was beating fast and her thoughts were in turmoil.

What will I do? Even if they didn't take my stuff, why are they acting in such a manner? Am I safe here?

She lay down on the bed and, despite her confusion, soon fell asleep, not waking until first light.

8 — Questions and Answers

'**The thief's name** was Jocko,' said Dominick. 'I can save you the trouble of interviewing him though.'

'How so?' asked Russell.

'Where's this all headed then?' The small, thickset man was easily holding Russell's hard stare.

'Can't see it's anything to do with you if I find out where the gold came from,' said Russell, nodding slowly and leaning forward ever so slightly.

Dominick went on to tell him the gold had come from the hotel room of a young Chinese geologist presently working for Exminoil. He claimed he'd fenced the stuff stolen from her, but denied knowing it was hot at the time. When Russell asked about her documents, Dominick had wiped the lank hair from his balding forehead and nodded as if agreeing. He maintained he'd never seen any of the bank cards, but said he could get hold of her passport and a few other bits and pieces which had no real value.

Russell agreed to call back in an hour to collect them and appeared surprised when Dominick referred to him as an employee of a surreptitious government department. The man had a fair idea who he worked for and he shouldn't have, not if he was simply the proprietor of a second hand goods store who fenced a bit of hot stuff now and then.

'Best if we forget we ever met afterwards,' said Russell before he closed the door of Dominick's office, unsure if his threat actually carried any weight with the man at all.

As soon as he got clear of Dominick's second-hand furniture store, Russell slipped out his mobile.

'So far so good Dave,' he replied after a few seconds, pausing to listen to his boss's greeting before continuing.

'The gold was stolen from a young Chinese geologist by the name of Siao Lin Wayne. I'll be getting her documents shortly. Credit cards are gone but you could trace them quick enough.'

He listened for ten or fifteen seconds, looking about as he walked along the concrete footpath, beneath the deep, red flowered limbs of an old Poinciana tree.

'Yeh,' he said. 'That Dominic character could do with watching, reckon he's a bit more than the research background I got suggested. I'll check the place where the gold was stolen from.'

At a T-junction he crossed the street and turned right, headed toward the town centre.

'Yeh, that'll be good,' he agreed after a few more seconds. 'I'll check my emails.'

Russell laughed at whatever Dave had said and smiled as cut the call. The phone was slipped back into his coat pocket as he turned a corner and passed the Coffs Hotel. He waited for the lights to change before crossing over the highway and into the central shopping area.

Two hours later, Russell half felt and half heard the mobile ringing.

'Russell.' He listened for nearly a minute before replying.

'Yeh. Got all that Dave,' he replied. 'Millar from Exminoil, I'll meet him at the Coffs at 8.30.'

'Nah. No luck up here. Got a bit of info on her, she left two days ago, without telling anyone where she was headed. I reckon that Dominick fellow knows something about the cobalt too.' As he listened to the conversation Russell frowned and shook his head.

'Just that he appears to have found a lot out in the hour between my visits. Should I work him over?'

'Yeh alright, I won't touch him. Be nice to know what's going on though. Maybe this Millar character will have more idea of where the girl is headed.'

'Sounds like some girl alright,' he nodded agreement and grinned. 'Email me if you get a trace on her cards. Catch you tomorrow Dave.'

Russell sat back in a lounge chair in the Coffs Hotel. He wasn't getting drunk, just enjoying a cold beer after a long hot day. He'd already spoken to Dave about his meeting with the Chief Geologist Peter Millar. The man had seemed genuine enough. They'd had an informal chat over a couple of steaks and a few beers.

Millar reckoned the girl had taken him totally by surprise. Her leaving so suddenly, within hours of receiving her new passport and licences, certainly seemed suspicious to Russell. When questioned about it, Millar had admitted knowing about the stolen gold, and it being high in cobalt. His company, Exminoil had told him, and yes they were somewhat interested. He'd not known the girl had been carrying any gold with her at all and wondered how it had not been detected when her hastily packed things had been shipped in from the rig.

Russell had the hollow dragon statuette which had been stolen from Siao Lin upstairs in his room, but didn't mention it. Gold inside bronze wouldn't have showed on scanners, a little heavy, but no-one would have noticed whilst it'd been inside a suitcase.

Why did the girl leave? Had she been planning to all along, and simply waited for her documents to arrive before vanishing? Seemed a logical assumption, but it didn't really fit in with the little he'd learned about her character so far. Russell had already checked with the bank. She'd taken out $10,000.00 the morning she left. The bank security video had shown him how nervous she was, there was certainly something worrying her. And why had she declined to mention the gold to the Police when asked what was stolen from her hotel room? Had she simply been worried about having brought it into the country illegally, or was her involvement actually deeper than it seemed?

If she used any of her cards, he'd be notified within minutes, but she could last a while on ten grand. She had definitely taken a plane to Sydney. Why? It'd been the only morning flight? She was probably in a hurry; she certainly didn't look comfortable in the surveillance videos. She took no other flights from Sydney, simply a bus to the city after which she'd vanished.

Russell had already told Dave of the leak from AMDEL, which had allowed information to slip through to Exminoil and who knows who else. Have to presume everybody knew, including Dominick who was definitely the type to waggle his fingers in any pie he came across. He'd requested Dave send up a couple of lads to keep an eye on him in the meantime.

He picked up the beer, downed it, thought about a whisky but stood and made his way up the carpeted stairs to his room. Time to sleep, the more questions he'd asked, the less he felt he knew about the Chinese girl, Siao Lin.

9 — Flashback

At eight o'clock, the morning after she'd heard Peter discussing her stolen gold on his phone, Siao Li ate breakfast in the small café at the resort, apart from a young couple she had the place to herself. Immediately after eating, she walked to a phone box and called Barry's wife. He was out driving, and had been since seven. She asked Maria to get him to come and pick her up as soon as it was convenient for him. Maria said she'd call the depot and arrange it.

Back in her room she quickly packed her things. A small case held everything she owned, apart from her new Australian passport, bank cards and cash which she kept in a slim shoulder bag.

Twenty minutes later Barry arrived. Siao Lin hired him for a half day, loaded her bag and they drove in to town where she did her bank business. She used her new cards, there were no problems at all now that she had her new Australian passport for ID, and took out a large amount of cash. She thought $10,000 should be enough to tide her over for a while.

Barry then drove her to the airport and as they pulled up in the unloading lane, she asked him not to tell anyone where he had taken her, at least for a day or two. She felt the need to vanish, but assured him she would be in touch once things had settled down and thanked him for all his help.

The first flight from the small airport was to Sydney. Adelaide was her real goal, from where she would eventually head north, but the flight to Sydney was the only one south that morning. She knew they could trace her easily enough on flights anyway and decided to simply take the first flight out, seeing it as a bonus not to be going direct to Adelaide.

From Sydney airport she took a bus to Central Railway Station, got a ticket there without needing to produce her ID. She spent several hours wandering around the harbour, ate in a small restaurant near circular quay and that evening at 8.40 caught a train to Melbourne. She seemed to notice cameras everywhere, but still felt she'd left too awkward a trail for anyone who was trying to track her.

Siao Lin slept in a narrow sleeping berth on the train, and once she became used to the swaying and that clacketty-clack railway noise, it was quite pleasant. The train arrived in Melbourne at 7.30 in the morning. If she had regrets about not seeing the scenery during the daylight hours, finding and catching the bus to Adelaide kept her too busy to worry about it.

After a long, tedious day of sitting in an uncomfortable bus seat and eating saggy take away food at the stops, she was relieved when the trip ended. The Firefly bus dropped her at the Adelaide Central Bus Station just before eight at night.

Worn and tired, she walked outside the terminal to hail a taxi. The night was already quite chilly, a few huddled up people passed by, but looked right through her. Siao Lin took the cab in search of an hotel. She thought they would have a hard time locating her if she didn't use her cards for a while, at least until she was nearly ready to travel on. This meant trying three hotels before finding one which didn't require her using ID. The room she rented had good secure looking locks and with windows too high to climb up to, she felt it a safe haven for the time being.

At last it seemed she could relax and continue with her plans to trace the route her ancestor had taken over a hundred years earlier. Determined to move the process on, she decided to visit the Department of Mines the following day and begin planning her trip. Using maps and geological plans, combined with the diary her great great grandfather had sent back to China, she should be able to ascertain where he had lived. Siao Lin couldn't help but wonder if she would also be able to locate the place he had found the gold. Despite her tiredness and a faint but lingering fear that she really was being sought by unknown villains, she was elated at being so close to exploring the dream she had sought since childhood. A childhood rich with the memories of the stories told, of her illustrious ancestor Tamo.

Tears of relief streaked her smooth, light brown, skin as she reached into her open case and removed the old parchment book.

Siao Lin dried the tears from her eyes began to read Tamo's diary, she scanned it as slowly and carefully as possible, in case there were hidden meanings within the old Chinese characters. She smiled at the way he started the writing, sensing a finality in the words which told her he well knew this was to be his last contact with the land of his birth.

May, 1857

In my youth it was said I had exceptional mental and physical skills and so was given to the Shaolin temple. That ancient structure stood on the only high ground in our area, offering a good view of the paddy fields beyond bamboo covered slopes. Most mornings, distant hump-backed hills sheared through layered mists like black and green islands in a pale sea of fog. On days when the mists cleared you could see the wide brown vastness of the Yellow River in the distance, but never to its far side.

The surrounding area consisted of rice paddies which would flood for several months each year, as the river spread itself across low lying lands to either side. The flooded fields were often used to grow shrimp and small fish which were netted as the paddies dried out and the rice neared harvesting.

I left the temple and married Soo Lin when I was twenty three. We set up house near her family's rice fields. I took employment occasionally as a guard to important personages, being well paid for my physical prowess. A fully trained Shaolin monk gave good protection from common thieves or footpads.

My last contract was to accompany a merchant to Shanghai City, which lay two full day's walk downriver. Several other men were also employed for his protection, but I was the only Shaolin. The others were just brawny ruffians, employed more for their brute strength and imposing size than for any actual skill.

On arrival at a house where the merchant was to meet with some foreigners, English men by the accents I overheard, we were asked to wait in a courtyard with high walls. I was hit heavily on the head from behind. One of the other guards employed along with me must have been responsible, for I heard no other approaching footstep.

I awoke in the prison cell, where for several months I languished, chained for the most part and allowed no contact, other than with fellow prisoners.

One of my meals must have been drugged, for some time later I awakened aboard an English vessel, already far out to sea. I was pressed into service as a labourer and a translator for the Chinese *passengers who were all travelling to Australia to search for gold. I was informed I would be released with the other passengers if I worked my passage and made no trouble.*

July, 1857

The small ship *tossed and pitched, after yet another storm, throwing the cramped passengers beneath decks about. The smell of unwashed bodies and vomit was momentarily blown from my face as I unlatched a small wooden porthole in an attempt to obtain some fresh air. My effort was rewarded by a dousing of icy salt water as the ship ploughed through another heavy swell.*

I heard the mate telling me to close the porthole, the Captain wanted to see me. I followed him and we weaved through the haphazardly sprawled bodies in the dim light.

Above decks the wet salt spray shone silver on his oilskin in the reflected lamplight. I followed close behind, ignoring the cold bite of the wind, which easily penetrated my thin cotton clothes. Sheets of icy spray sleeted, wind-blown across the deck, stinging like needles, as the vessel plunged down one huge wave and into the face of the next.

I dropped willingly into the hard wooden chair in the Captain's cabin. Salt water dripped from my clothes and little pools formed about my sandaled feet on the rough wooden floorboards.

The Captain told me to tell the passengers they'd be landed just before first light and to have them to pack their belongings and be ready. He told me I could row in with the crew and would be free once I'd been landed. I could hear the lie in his voice but was unsure just what the truth was.

Back below deck, I spread word that we were near the end of the voyage. Reaction to the news was heartening and, despite my lingering suspicion, infectious. Exchanging the ever moving splintery floors for the solidarity of dry land and a chance at riches in the newly discovered Australian goldfields had buoyed attitudes and expectations of all the would be miners.

During the voyage I had scrubbed decks, sewn netting, spliced rope and the like. Not that I minded, for I had spent far more time above decks than the others trapped below-decks. Despite the poor diet aboard ship, it seemed I would arrive in Australia in good condition, if a bit on the lean side.

Later, as every other Chinese man aboard celebrated, I was morose. My thoughts flew to the Temple where I'd trained in my youth as a warrior priest. Inward discipline had been instilled to forge my will. Despite inner strength, I had experienced dire misfortune when the patron I had been well paid to protect had been murdered. The plot, probably orchestrated by the British, had involved even those guards I had trusted. I tried to see beyond the men who lied and enforced their will upon me, to make allowances for the zeal with which they seemed to carry out their harsh orders.

I had thoughts also of my wife and children, but did not dwell on those memories for long. That way lay madness. I had been told in no uncertain terms, if ever I returned to China all their lives would be forfeit, I would never see them again.

10 — Dominick

Russell Gibb had left a few minutes before Dominic heard a tap on the door. Rabbit's head popped into view.

'Big Frank's here Dom.'

Dominick, who'd been thinking to send for Frank a few seconds earlier, gestured for Rabbit to show him in. Frank walked in, freshly shaved head tanned brown and looking tough as mahogany.

'Dom,' he nodded.

'Sit down Frank,' said Dominic, gesturing open handed.

Frank's smile was fleeting.

'Just had a tough looking nut named Russell Gibb call, asking me questions about the gold that Rabbit took from a girl's room at the Park Beach. He walked off toward town about two minutes ago.'

'What's he wearing?' Frank was already standing and moving toward the door.

'Jeans and a pale blue shirt,' said Dominick, waving him away. 'You'll know him. Looks like a pro'.'

'Saw him walking,' nodded Frank as he opened the door. 'Organisation?'

'Could be.' Dominick agreed. 'Get back to me as soon as you have anything.'

By the time Frank had closed the door, Dominick had already called a number. He spoke to Glenn, a hacker he used at times, told him what he knew and asked him to find out what he could.

Dominick stood up and walked to the window as he dialled another number.

'Bill, this is Dominick, how are you?' Dominick walked back to his desk and sat down.

'Oh nothing important Bill. I just had a visit from Russell Gibb and thought I'd check up on him. Does he actually work for you?'

As Dominick listened a grin lit his face. He made a fist with his free hand and punched the air with it.

'That bad is he?' said Dominick grinning like a crocodile as he picked up a pen and began scribbling.

'The gold? No I don't really know anything about it. Heard it was nicked alright, but that's it. Let me know how it pans out will you

Bill.'

'She flew to Sydney then did she?' Dominick was still grinning. 'She must know they're after her eh?'

He told Bill to email him if any further developments arose, put the phone into his pocket and walked into the shop. He sent Rabbit for a long lunch and wandered about the store. He'd a hunch there was something pretty solid going on and he meant to be in on it.

Dominick had long since sent Rabbit home for the evening when Frank arrived back. The big man followed him into the office and they both sat down.

'How'd you go?' asked Dominick.

Frank nodded, he looked quite pleased with himself. He described how he'd witnessed a meeting between Russell and Peter Millar, a geologist from Exminoil. They'd talked about the girl, how the gold was high in cobalt and Exminoil were very interested in its source. Frank mentioned that Peter Millar had been taken completely by surprise at her running off.

'Did Russell go anywhere else?' asked Dominick.

'He called to the Park Beach Hotel, the Police Station and then drove off somewhere in a hire car. Not sure where he went, time I got to my car he was gone.'

Dominick hired Frank to search for the girl, gave him all the information he'd gained from Bill and Glenn. He didn't mention the conversation he'd had with the security reps from a Chinese mining giant Zihnjihn, who were so interested in his information they offered him up front cash to investigate. Dodgy bastards, but if they were paying, he'd take their cash. He gave Frank Glenn's number and even Bill's just in case.

Frank queried who Bill was.

'He's our insider,' said Dominic evenly. 'Make sure you cover your tracks, he's organisation. But he's come up with the goods on this one so far; seems to have a grudge against this Russell character. There'll be a big payday if we can get the location of this gold before the Organisation does.'

'The Organisation though?' asked Frank. 'Is Glenn that good?'

Dominick just nodded. He didn't tell Frank, Glenn had already got a lot of information from an analysis company called AMDEL – Australian Mineral Developmental Laboratories – information about the gold and its high cobalt content. Glenn had told him the traffic was heavy in two ways. Lots of traffic and it seemed the US Government had an interest too.

'Usual rates then?' asked Frank.

Dominick handed Frank an envelope containing cash and another with a grainy photograph of Siao Lin. He told him to go to Sydney and see if he could find the girl. Frank didn't say anything, simply stood, pushed his chair in and turned for the door.

'One more thing Frank, I'd better mention this.' Dominick was grinning as Frank turned back. 'The girl is definitely more than she seems. Three men attacked her on an offshore rig she was working on. She killed one and disabled the other two.'

'That's what Russell Gibb and Millar were talking about when they mentioned two men who are looking for her too. They're still in Coffs, think she's here somewhere.' Frank was smiling.

Dominick rubbed his chin as he thought for a few seconds.

'See if you can locate them before you go,' he added.

Frank nodded.

'Hire them if you can.' Dominick watched Frank across his desk. 'Their lust for revenge'll be a good smokescreen. Get them to do your dirty work, they're expendable.'

Frank nodded, Dominick saw the faintest trace of distaste flash across his features. He stood and turned away toward the door.

He doesn't want to work with them thought Dominick, but then, neither would I.

It didn't take Frank long to locate the driller and his offsider. They'd been asking so many questions they'd left a trail as wide as the Pacific Highway.

He noticed the younger man still had an arm in plaster as the two entered a seedy coffee shop for a cheap breakfast. He followed them in.

'Heard you're looking for a Chinese girl,' Frank said, walking up to them as soon as they'd taken their seats.

'You heard right,' said the older man, standing up to a height almost on a level with Frank. Tattoos adorned his arms and his T-shirt was clean but threadbare. 'Do you know where she is?'

'Know where she went from here,' replied Frank.

'Wada' you want then?'

'Name's Frank,' he said extending a hand. The man looked down at his hand, then back to his face before sitting back down.

'I want to hire you,' said Frank, ignoring the slight. 'Don't care about the girl, just need to find her.'

'What's this about then?' asked the younger man, the one with his arm in plaster.

'The girl has information my employer needs,' he admitted. 'I'll pay you a hundred dollars a day each plus expenses. She flew out to Sydney two days ago.'

'Ah shit,' muttered the younger man. 'Told you she was gone.'

'Cash?' asked the other man, ignoring his mate.

Frank nodded.

'We'll sign up then,' said the older man. 'My name's Roy and this one armed lad answers to Kid.

They spent a week in Sydney, but despite a lot of looking came up with nothing. The girl had apparently vanished into a teeming population of over three million, spread out over twelve thousand square kilometres. They were lazing about in their motel room near the airport when Big Frank took a call from Glenn. He'd hacked into a computer of one of the organisation's employees and pulled out an email; a notification of the use of the girl's debit card. She'd bought a car in Adelaide the previous day.

Frank rang the airport, booked the three of them on a flight to Adelaide which departed in an hour's time and called a cab.

'Pack up boys,' he said. 'We're off to Adelaide. Girl's been found.'

Neither of the two men said anything but he could see they were still determined to go through with their revenge despite his warning them. He knew they couldn't be let near the girl, and he'd no illusions as to what they'd do if it suited them. Sooner he was rid of them the better; Dom must have known how useless they'd be, worse than bloody useless. He threw his clothes into the suitcase and they were gone the moment they heard the cab's horn outside.

11 — Adelaide

The morning after she arrived in Adelaide, Siao Lin was in no mood to put things off. She visited the Department of Mines and arranged for a miner's right, just in case she found where the gold came from and needed to stake a claim. After speaking with a young geologist at the sales counter, she figured the northern Flinders Ranges was the most likely area her ancestor could have gone. She purchased both geological and topographical maps to cover the whole of the area; even had a cursory glance at them. Nothing jogged her memory. She felt a little flat, her mood of high expectation slipping into vague disappointment.

Later, in the early afternoon, she sat on a park bench in dappled sunshine; faded autumn leaves tugged loose by a fitful breeze punctuated the cool air. The song of a young boy playing guitar and singing nearby was pleasant and relaxing. She couldn't catch all the words at first but found when she concentrated, clarity crystallised as the volume appeared to swell.

> 'Daydreams drifting into sand,
> seagulls calling life a lie,
> surf still roars into my ears,
> sunlight finds my eyes…'

The song was still being played, she was listening, but it seemed such a long way off. Like a dream, she thought. My eyes are closed, can I open them? She didn't quite open them, yet was suddenly looking between the thick white trunks of two ancient gum trees. Beyond, some distance away, a black skinned youth sat on a dry, gravelly riverbed.

He looked up and swatted a fly away. He was abruptly closer, looking at her intently.

'I know you," he said, grinning.

His teeth were too white. Two white cockatoos uttered harsh screeches as they swerved around the course of the meandering creekbed. She glimpsed bright yellow feathers standing up from their heads as they turned sharply and slipped out of sight behind rearing walls of fractured red quartzite.

'We share blood,' he said, gazing at her. His eyes were black.

'Where is this?' she asked out of interest, not feeling at all worried, just confused. Somehow, deep inside, she knew this was a vision, but interest turned her head and the mountains were so clear and bright she was forced to squint.

'This dreamtime,' the youth laughed again. 'My world, but you're welcome too.'

Siao Lin grinned at the clarity of the scene. Red rocks, even the leaves had red tips. The landscape beyond the youth looked sharp and barren, the creekbed, dry and rocky, had steep banks cut into a greenish tinged bed of what appeared to be weathered calc-silicate rock.

'Where are you?' she asked. Though basically the same question, it seemed important.

'You dream me again at Paralana,' he laughed and lifted a hand in farewell.

The scene flickered away. Siao Lin heard the song, distant, but it had always been there. She glimpsed a rugged chain of mountains from above, before the music strengthened and her eyes flicked open. The same song was still being played, she noticed how bright and vibrant the park's autumn colours were as the song finished.

Must've been a short dream. Paralana? Wonder where that is?

As the song finished several aborigines, who'd been sitting in a group near a thicket of green bushes, walked down and sat on the grass by the boy. They talked. She thought the boy gave them some money. She felt tired and again closed her eyes.

She heard soft footsteps and opened her eyes to find one of the aborigines sitting on the end of the bench, looking at her.

She nodded to him and smiled faintly, it was too nice a day not to.

'Can you give us a coupla' bob girley?' He asked, not at all threatening. She could smell smoke and alcohol.

'You going to buy drink?' She asked, already reaching into her bag.

'Food too,' he admitted, smiling.

She passed him a few dollar coins.

'You might be my cousin,' said the man as he stood, grinning with white teeth as he leaned forward to take the change. 'My ancestor also Chinese man.'

'When?' she asked suddenly feeling a lot more awake.

'Long time ago,' he continued to smile. 'Back when white man first come here. You go Nepabunna. I back there next week. Come see me there. I tell you where to go. He stay at Adnyamathanha when most of tribe leave. That where he lived, and where he died too.'

He nodded his thanks and was gone, his two companions walking away with him. They joined the rest of the group from the bushes, and all headed across the park to the nearest pub.

Paralana, Nepabunna and Adnyamathanha. Three names.

Siao Lin felt buoyed by the fruits of an unlikely coincidence. She picked up her bags and walked back through busy city streets.

Back in her hotel room, she looked through the maps she'd purchased and found all three names. They were in similar areas, although Nepabunna was quite a distance further south. Adnyamathanha was spelled as Yudnamutana. As she continued looking across the table at the plans she suddenly saw a name which struck the final note of a complex chord. Wheal Frost, her ancestor had mentioned the same name in his diary. It was of one of the copper mines he'd been near.

She examined the tracks on the map, they were dotted red lines and on checking the legend she discovered they were four wheel drive tracks. If I'm alone up there I'll need to be well equipped. She took out a writing pad and paper and began to make a list of what she thought she'd need.

Next morning she hailed a taxi and asked the driver to take her to a car dealer who had good four wheel drive vehicles. Both the taxi driver and the salesman she spoke to told her that Toyota Landcruisers were the best if the country got rough. She took their advice and purchased one with an extra fuel tank and a built in water tank as well. It was second hand but appeared to be sturdy and reliable.

Though she knew it was risky using her bank card, she took the chance. She'd be leaving Adelaide within a few days and had to give the dealer a name and an address to complete the purchase anyway.

At a large outdoor store in Thebarton, she purchased lots of other gear including, two jerry-cans, digging and mining tools, a good strong tent and camp mattress, blankets, along with a fishing rod the shop assistant assured her would work well.

Relaxed and relieved she'd accomplished so much so quickly, Siao Lin ate a light salad for lunch and drank orange juice in a small café near the river. She walked along the riverbank, under an old steel framed bridge. Small paddle boats passed by as she sat on a shady bench and watched a mother duck seeing to her brood of tiny black and yellows chicks.

She watched a man approach, not really taking much notice of him until he stopped on the path in front of her.

'Hi Siao Lin,' he said, squatting down. 'My name is Russell Gibb, I work for the Federal Government, and I need to talk to you.'

12 — Flown

'**Sorry to intrude** on such a lovely evening,' I continued. 'We've recovered some of your documents and I'd like to return them to you.'

Siao Lin watched me, easily holding my eyes. She didn't look particularly impressed; if looks could do damage.

'Russell?' she asked, still holding my eyes. 'Exactly who did you say you worked for?'

'I mentioned the Federal Government,' I said clearly. I'm also supposed to keep an eye on you,' the words were out before I realised it might have been better to leave telling her some things until later.

'These belong to you.' I passed across a clear plastic wallet. She looked down at it, slipped it open and pulled the contents free.

'My Chinese passport,' she looked up and almost smiled. 'My cards were all cancelled, but the passport would have taken a long time to replace.'

'This is yours too.' I handed across the stubby brass dragon I drew out of my pocket.

Siao Lin took the statue and hefted it, obviously judging the weight.

I told her I didn't want to invade her privacy, mentioned that some rather unsavoury characters were seeking her and suggested that maybe I could help. She said she didn't need or want my help and reckoned she'd be happier if I just went away.

I thought about the way she'd protected herself on the rig in New Guinea and mentioned something about it, adding that I had been given a job and needed to carry it out. She asked me if it was about the gold and I admitted it was. She said emphatically that she didn't know where her ancestor found the gold and didn't really care. I believed her but knew there were things she wasn't telling me too.

She asked me to leave her alone again, easy to tell she meant it.

'Sorry to bother you Siao Lin,' I said, standing and looking down at her, time for a tactical retreat. 'It was nice to finally meet you.'

I spent a long night waiting in a beaten up old Ford Falcon panel van, watching Siao Lin's hotel. It was bloody cold, and anyway, I'd more or less decided she'd left before I arrived, sometime in the afternoon. My latest instructions from Bill were to wait, so I kept on waiting. By that time the car was getting pretty warm in the sun, even with the windows down. About the time I was debating whether or not to go up and confirm my suspicions, I noticed three men approaching from behind the car.

The tallest of the three was wearing a close fitting tracksuit and the others were dressed in scruffy Levis and T-shirts. I watched them in the mirror.

Shit! I thought, that looks like the guy who was in the Coffs Hotel when I was talking to the geologist from Exminoil. They walked past the car and crossed the street to enter the hotel. The tall man turned to survey the area. I took a shot of him with my phone and sent it off to the office. He seemed to be staring at the car and me. The other two waited, appearing impatient. The one with the plaster on one arm said something.

The man I'd recognised stared at the car a few seconds longer before turning and following the other two inside.

I phoned the office. It was picked up before the second ring. Bill answered it.

'Put me through to Dave Bill.' I said.

'No, you can't deal with it Bill,' I said a few seconds later. 'Put me through to Dave please.'

'Hi Dave. Same guy who was sitting near me when I interviewed Peter Millar has just turned up with a couple of rough looking characters. They just walked into the hotel.'

'Likely she's gone. Left yesterday. Bill told me to hang around here.'

Dave told me to confront the guy and tell him to back off. Protocol, need to warn the bastards first. I agreed. He asked if I needed backup, I said I didn't.

It was a lot cooler outside the car, winter wasn't too far away. I walked to the hotel entrance, a shady piece of wall looked cool, so I leaned on it. A few seconds later the big bald goon and his two scruffy friends walked out.

'Can I have a few words,' I said as the big man spotted me.

He turned to his two henchmen. I could see they were shaping to have a go at me already, obviously not professionals by any stretch of the imagination.

'I'll see you at the car in a minute or two lads,' he said, placing a hand on each of their shoulders and gently pushing them down the last two steps.

He turned back to face me and nodded faintly. 'Your mob's on the ball then eh Russell.'

'Boss told me to warn you off.' I took a step toward him.

'Names Frank,' he said, not moving. 'Big Frank. Consider me warned then,'

He didn't smile, but I could see he wasn't going to back off.

'You workin' for Dominic then?' Wasn't such a long shot.

'Not your business Russ.' He confirmed my suspicion by not denying it. I held back.

'It's a free world isn't it?' Now he was smiling.

'Might be free back in Ireland Frank,' I grinned at him. 'But you aren't so big over here.'

'We finished?' he asked.

'Nearly,' I asked. 'Who're the goons then?'

'You don't need to worry about them Russ,' he seemed amused. 'They couldn't even hurt the girl.'

I told him what I thought of his compatriots. He laughed and admitted that he had his orders too. I reckoned he was good and wanted to try him out but knew I couldn't.

He didn't walk away though, our eyes remained locked.

'Be better if we don't meet again too soon Frank,' I said as I turned my back and walked to the car. Needed to get back to the office. I might be a bloody good swimmer, but leaky boats have never appealed to me.

Back at the office Dave had already matched the photo I'd sent in to Big Frank aka Frank Wingston, a native of Dublin. He was rumoured to have had IRA connections in the past and had certainly served as a military advisor and mercenary in Africa. He had no known criminal record but had done some sub-contract work for our government in the past.

'He's worked for the Organisation?' I said to Dave. Why wasn't I surprised?

'Who is Dominic then?' I asked.

'Just local Mafiosi,' replied Dave. 'Used to be a big wheel in Sydney but seems to be more or less retired in Coffs Harbour these days. He obviously feels there's cash to be made in this deal.'

'I don't like working in the dark at the best of time,' I said looking Dave in the eyes. I needed what he wasn't telling. 'When it's you pulling the wool Dave, I'm apt to get a bit pissed.'

He said nothing.

'What else?' I kept my voice even.

Dave just shook his head. There was no reply.

'I can't do my job if important information... Pertinent information is withheld.'

'He was a contact we used at times,' admitted Dave.

'He used to do hits for us?' I said in disbelief. 'I figured he'd sussed who I was working for, but... You shoulda' told me before you sent me to him. What's going on?'

Dave blamed Bill for the shoddy intelligence I'd received and added that he had already been censured for it.

With a good idea of where the leak was I cut off his excuse, accusing him of looking the other way because Bill was his wife's brother. He gave me a hard look and asked if I wanted off the job. I knew he was serious. I wanted the job. That girl had already intrigued me, I just wanted to know what I was up against.

I told him I wanted the job but asked him not to give Bill any further information concerning the girl. I suggested he check all Bill's phone calls and get the IT guys onto seeing his emails were still secure. Big Frank's arrival meant we definitely had some sort of leak. Maybe Bill's connection with Dominic was too obvious, but then again, was he smart enough to do it any other way. I knew Dave would have to run some checks once I'd gone on the record. It made me a little happier.

'Okay Russ, I'll look into it,' he continued when I'd finished my tirade. 'Anyway, Siao Lin's used her bank card to extract money yesterday afternoon. Then her car was picked up by a roadside camera headed out on the Melbourne freeway yesterday afternoon. Last heard of at Keith, could be headed for Melbourne.'

'Got any more info about the gold?' I asked. 'She knew more than she told me. Even if the gold was sent to China last century, I feel she knows a bit more about its general location.'

'Hmmm,' said Dave, nodding. 'Funny you should ask that. All in your dossier.'

He handed a folder across the table.

I looked at the folder, but made no attempt to pick it up. I looked back at Dave, waiting.

'There were specks of bedrock with the gold,' he said, shaking his head at my theatrics. 'It wasn't enough to do much with, but they reckon it came from somewhere between Victor Harbour and the northern Flinders Ranges. Big area, but it can't be from where the girl has headed.'

'What's she driving?' asked Russell.

'Toyota Landcruiser, it's fitted with an extra long-range tank.'

'I'll need the Cayenne.'

Dave opened his top drawer and threw the extracted set of keys.

I caught the keys and stood, scooping up the dossier.

'I'll be in touch,' I said as I turned to leave.

I turned at the door and grinned at Dave. 'You'll likely have a few speeding fines to cover.' Be out of character if I didn't say something smart.

13 — Robe

Siao Lin watched Russell walk away without looking back, surprised at her feelings, for despite a little fear and a strong dislike at his intrusion, she somehow felt he was a man to be trusted and one she wouldn't mind getting to know better. I'll leave tonight, she thought, the faintest of smiles fleeting across the edges of her lips. I've no reason to stay here any longer. In fact I've a good reason not to; if he could find me, others can too.

She walked up the hill toward the city and turned left, along South Terrace. A few leaves spiralled down in the building afternoon breeze as Siao Lin gazed absently up at the spiky, near naked branches overhead. She moved off and kicked her way through heavy drifts of autumn leaves along the edge of the pathway.

She wandered around a bit, and finally arrived back at her hotel around 5 pm. In her room, she studied a local map, figuring out her intended route, packed her small bag and sneaked out, down the fire-escape stairs. Her Toyota Landcruiser was already loaded with the gear she'd purchased earlier in the day. She skirted the city, drove along the edge of the parklands eastward, toward the Melbourne freeway, only stopping to use her bank card to take out some cash. The start of her false trail, she thought. Her destination was north, but she'd firstly explore the place where her ancestor came ashore.

As she drove, Siao Lin wondered how much of the surveillance stuff she'd seen in American movies recently was real. Many of the films she'd watched on board the drilling platform had featured so many ways of locating and tracking people. Her use of her own name and address when she purchased the car had probably led Russell to her. Yet he seemed no threat, maybe he really did work for the government, but she wasn't going to suddenly start trusting a stranger. And anyway, she had really had no idea exactly where the gold came from. There shouldn't have been any in the areas her grandfather had been in, she had already established that by studying the geology of the area on her maps.

The big 4 wheel drive, with its V8 diesel made easy work of the long motorway climb up into the Adelaide hills. Several times she noticed camera-like devices on the roadside. Radar or surveillance cameras, she wondered? By the time Siao Lin crossed the Murray River she'd decided she wasn't going to make it too easy for them to track her. The road she was on led to Melbourne. Once they thought she was headed there she should be able to simply vanish.

After Tailem Bend, rather than turn off on the Princess Highway, the road to her next destination, she kept following the Duke's Highway, the quickest way to Melbourne.

An hour later, at a busy service station, with lots of CCTV cameras, she filled both her 90 litre tanks and the two extra jerry-cans with diesel. She paid with her bank card again and made a point of asking the girl serving how long it would take to get to Melbourne.

The main street ran off the highway at right angles and the local fish and chip shop was easy to find. It had been about to close, but the proprietor was friendly and cooked her some grilled flathead with salad. She ate as he wound down the shop for the night. He seemed a nice old man and she regretted having to lie to him about where she was going, but it didn't seem to be too harmful and was possibly necessary.

Siao Lin drove out of town, still headed SE, toward Melbourne. Three kilometres further on she turned right, onto a side road named Stirling Road, which cut through to the Naracoorte Road. It was a narrow and likely too small and insignificant to have any roadside cameras. Hopefully, she had effectively disappeared. She would try and hide her trail; thankfully she wouldn't need to use credit cards in the near future.

She skirted the town of Kingston an hour and a half later, bemused at the huge lobster on the roadside. She chose the Lobster Motel for accommodation and signed on with an anglicised version of her name, Sue Wayne, paid cash and gave a somewhat different registration number from her actual one. Her room was at the rear, away from the highway and her vehicle would be hidden from passing traffic. She locked her door carefully and felt slightly nervous about sleeping in yet another new place for all of thirty seconds before she fell into a deep and dream-filled sleep.

The following morning Siao Lin rose early and swam for about half an hour in the motel pool. She ate a light breakfast in a small café in the town centre and wandered up and down the main street, leisurely looking at the shops. On her return to the motel she packed her bag and headed south.

The drive to Robe was flat and uneventful. Her first stop was to visit the beach on the seaward side of the town, where her ancestor had first landed. She was amazed at the craggy stone of the beach. She'd read her great, great grandfather's words so many times and never imagined he had come ashore in such a wicked looking place. Jagged reefs rose clear of the water in numerous places, and even the beach was mostly water worn stone, with pebbly sand in a few places.

She imagined a Corporal sitting his horse patiently in a cold damp wind, on a cold dark beach, nearly a hundred and forty years previously. He'd have been thankful the rain had stopped. The ship would've been barely visible off the dark, rocky coast. They were lying to, probably disembarking Chinese miners in the darkness. She envisaged twenty troopers huddled around a small, hidden fire, until the lookout atop the cliffs sighted longboats leaving the ship, mere shadows in the moonlight across a roiling sea. The troopers would have spread out across the beach, looking forward to a hot breakfast in Robe once the illegal immigrants were locked safely behind bars.

Siao Lin reached into her bag and extracted her ancestor's diary. She sat on a stone ledge above the thin stretch of sand and shingle. As she took a deep breath of fresh sea air, she began reading at the point the longboats left the ship.

14 — Landing

July, 1854

As we rowed toward shore, I watched the sailors heed the bowman's cries, pulling hard on oars to avoid jagged teeth-like rocks. I listened to the curses of the sailors; they cursed the rocks and the waves; they cursed the night's darkness and the load of chinks for whom they unwillingly risked their skins. I was just wondering whether they would speak so freely if they knew I understood them, when a piece of banter chilled me more than the sea-spray laden wind which gusted across the longboat.

One sailor mentioned finding solace in the fact that those responsible for this hairy trip to the shore and back would soon be arrested.

I stood up and continued rowing, searching the darkness ahead for the beach. I thought I saw a thin ribbon of pale sand beyond the waves as they broke away from us. I felt a large wave rising up behind, lifting the boat as it reared. Initially, the longboat began to slip violently sideways, but the rudder man reacted quickly and the steering oar lessened the slewing. Riding the wave in to the shore would speed the trip and hoard some of the rowers' strength for the return journey. I added a push with my legs to the sharp turning of the boat and was flung upwards and out, overboard and crashing, with an icy shock, into the freezing embrace of a dark, churning sea.

My bundle, sealed well and of waxed cotton, popped me to the surface after a few seconds. The boat was already out of sight behind the back of the wave it had caught. Moonlight suddenly lit the sea, it'd picked a good time to appear from behind dark, scudding clouds. I couldn't see the beach, but there were dim, looming shapes close by; jagged silhouettes of sharp and wicked looking rocks.

I splashed toward them, not waiting to be swept away by the next wave. My hands grasped and gripped sharp barnacle encrusted rocks as the wall of water crashed over me. Hanging on was only possible because the rock itself dissipated most of the wave's force. I was cut and scratched as I scrabbled for purchase. I had to readjust my grip, and was bleeding from numerous cuts before I managed to wedge myself into a narrow crack and inch my way upward. Several more waves crashed over me, until I'd scrambled high enough for only spray from the surf to reach me. I watched from a cold wet perch as the last streamers of thin cloud swept clear of the fat crescent moon and saw the shadowy forms of troopers moving about the beach, herding their captives. The sailors rowed their craft back out without mishap, the troopers hadn't appeared to have any interest in them.

By the time the prisoners were rounded up and marched through the dunes at the back of the beach, the vessel I'd arrived on had sailed from sight, and the morning light was starting to bring the rugged coastline to life. Amazed at how tortured the rocks appeared, I knew I had been lucky to have escaped with so few cuts and scratches.

I'd spent much of my childhood swimming in the swollen yellow river, so the short distance to the beach held no fears. I swam it and was indeed glad to finally feel sand and shingle under my feet. Just beyond the reach of the waves lay a body, I had not been the only one to go overboard.

I had no compunction about rifling the dead man's pockets and taking the pack from his back. I gained several sealed packets of seed, three sharp knives and a flint, fishing twine and cotton, along with several new steel fish hooks. What he had brought with him would serve me well. I had so little and felt very alone on that unknown shore.

I noticed several large scavenging birds circling overhead. They would attract attention and unsure of where the nearby town was, I opted to return to the seashore. I walked along the beach to where rocky buttresses of sharp sandy stone rose high above the thin strip of rock and coarse sand. Caves and cracks abounded in the area and I hid myself away from the light of day.

Just after sunset, I moved cautiously around the coast, following a long shelf of hard rocky sandstone. I got down to the sea at one point and found the rock pools abounded with shellfish, crabs and small fish which I took with my hands and ate raw. I was grateful for the food and felt some strength begin to return to my body.

Later, in the dead of night, I came to a place where a light beacon fended ships from a rugged promontory. From there on, the coastline turned back on itself. The scrub covered cliffs lessened in height as I walked, and gradually the roar of breaking waves diminished to separate sharp, shingly slaps. I had turned into a bay, protected from the onslaught of the breakers. An hour or so later I saw lights in the distance, smelled the smoke of fires and heard dogs barking. I could venture little further in that direction lest I risk discovery.

Fortune intervened again and had me stumble across a small dingy, drawn up high on a narrow, shingle clad beach. I borrowed it without a second thought, rowing across the mouth of the broad but protected bay. I had already decided to head west rather than to the east, where they might well seek for me. As I rowed quietly across the calm stretch of water, the moon had set and the phosphorescence was astonishing; I had neither seen the like before, nor since. Each fish in the sea seemed to radiate vast amounts of light and even the blades of the oars I used were flashing so brightly, I felt sure I would be seen. I wasn't, for I made land on the western end of a sandy beach, pulling the boat as far up from the sea as I could, so it would be found the next day. There were three or four hours of darkness remaining.

My eyes were so used to the dark that even in the starlight I managed to locate some tasty shellfish. I drank a small amount of water from my skin, I would need to find water the following day. By sunup I had reached a low rocky headland, beyond which the shore turned from north to west. I sheltered amongst the rocks rather than walk the next long sandy beach beyond in daylight.

I slept most of the day and began walking after sunset. My initial idea had been to walk for three days and cover what distance I could, so I pressed on through the darkness. I had eaten well of crabs and shellfish in the rocks, it seemed food abounded. I walked around another rocky headland, luckily the moon was rising earlier and I had welcomed its light to get across the rocks.

The beach beyond was a welcome break, but several hours before daybreak I realised I had reached a large town. Rather than skirt around the back of it, I opted to follow the beach. Several times, dogs barked as I passed, but none came after me. A small freshwater stream crossed my path and on hearing voices, I was forced to walk out into deeper water to cross the channel of the stream. I waited nearby in the lee of a damaged boat and soon the men walked away upstream and into the town. I drank deeply, and began filling my *waterskin, which was small, holding only enough for a day or two at best. On the spur of the moment I decided to use the bag I had taken from the dead man to hold my goods, allowing me to fill my waxed cotton bag with water. This was heavy but it gave me several extra days of water.*

After reading, Siao Lin put the old diary away and drove around the edge of the cliffs to where a white marker stood to warn ships. The cliffs at that point were far higher, not climbable at all. Further around, where a jetty stood out into the protected waters of the bay, is where Tamo must have borrowed the dingy and crossed the water to avoid the town.

Next she drove to the long sandy beach where he must have landed the boat and commenced his long walk. Siao Lin walked a few kilometres along the shore, looking at shells and watching the waves dump onto the sand.

On return to her car she followed the coast as well as she could, reaching Kingston just after midday. This must have been where her ancestor had taken fresh water from the stream and had been forced to swim to avoid detection. By the afternoon she had driven to where the Coorong was over a kilometre wide.

15 — Encounter

The Cayenne made short work of the freeway to the Murray. I slowed to around the state speed limit once the roads narrowed. I was over a day behind and there was no real rush.

By the time I crossed the Murray River it was obvious the bike behind was tailing me. At Tailem bend I pulled into the first service station and filled the car. It only took a few dollars of diesel. I paid and got a can of coke, walked to the car and headed off.

Before I even cleared the town the bike was a couple of cars behind again, been waiting up the second side street. Total bloody amateur.

Ten kilometres later, still on the Melbourne road, I did a sudden turn to the left onto a narrow dirt road. The bike missed the turn, but I saw him turn on the highway and come back. The dust cloud behind meant I couldn't see him, but I figured he'd be a few hundred metres behind, clear of the dust, where he could still see. Several kilometres later, at a T junction, I spun the monster and turned around, headed back the way I'd come at speed.

As expected, no sooner had I cleared the dust than the bike was headed at me. The rider just had time to slow and pull off, across the shoulder and into tall grass and dry thistles. I swerved straight at him in the last seconds. The large Porsche skidded sideways, knocking the rider off the bike as it stopped. A swirl of dust passed as I jumped out of the door in a second, gun already held down by my side. The rider, who had one arm in a plaster, was struggling to rise and hold on to his injured leg at the same time.

He was never going to get up, I could see the leg was broken. Even without the plaster on his arm, I'd recognised him. He'd been one of the two scruffs with Frank yesterday. Maybe he wasn't much more than a big kid but he was man enough to be trying to do harm to the girl I was meant to be looking after.

'What's your name?' I asked slowly as the youth looked up, face screwed up with the pain.

An hour later I drove into the service station where Siao Lin had used her card. I'd phoned Dave just after I'd left my tail floundering in the dust beside his crumpled bike, there'd been no further trace of her since the previous day. The same girl I spoke to had served Siao Lin and indeed remembered her well enough. She'd said she was Melbourne bound and had indeed headed off in that direction.

I ambled on through Bordertown and noticed no cameras of any use. At Kaniva I stopped at the NAB branch, and after a brief conversation and document production session with the manager, examined the CCTV footage for the previous evening. It was dark when I'd assured myself she hadn't passed that way, the manager had agreed to hang about. I thanked him and headed back to Keith, wondering which way she'd headed.

I phoned the office again and told them. Bill called back later and told me the gold couldn't be from anywhere near where I was, the telluride balance was all wrong. I booked in to the hotel, had a few pints with a steak and got to sleep early. It was as good a place as any to stay.

The following morning I checked a camera on the Melbourne side of Keith and found she had gone out of town in that direction alright, so she'd turned off somewhere between Keith and Bordertown.

I started taking roads at random and asking after her vehicle but nothing half way definite turned up. I returned to Keith the following night, ate a similar steak, drank twice as much of the same beer and slept in the same lumpy bed.

I got a call as I was finishing a breakfast of bacon and toast. She'd used her card again. Twice in fact, at Mannum, barely an hour previously. I jumped into the Porsche and was in Mannum around forty minutes later. Story from the attendant was that she'd said she was headed to Adelaide.

I wondered though. She seemed to like telling people where she was going and then not actually going there. She was leading me around. Where had she been for two days? Where was she going?

I took the Adelaide Road again; sure she'd at least left by that route. Just before the river, I took the turn off for Murray Bridge, why not, good as any other road. I spent the rest of the day asking around the town and checked a couple of cameras. There was no sign she'd come that way at all.

Rather than spend another fruitless night in a country town, I went back to Adelaide and stayed in a decent hotel, sure, the government could afford it. I reckoned maybe she'd gone for the gold and just hoped we found her before whoever else was looking did. I really thought she'd turn up, but I was wrong, she'd vanished for the time being.

16 — Northward

Siao Lin booked into a motel at Tailem bend, ate in a little café, spoke to the waitress about looking forward to getting back to Adelaide and went to bed early. In the morning she paid the motel bill with her bank card. She re-filled her car, topping up both tanks, and again used her card to pay at the service station. Siao Lin drove out of town, hoping her deception would set any pursuit off in the wrong direction.

Before crossing over the Murray, she turned off on the old Princess Highway toward Murray Bridge. She skirted Murray Bridge itself and drove along the road on the eastern side of the river. From time to time she would follow dead end tracks down to where the brown river swirled about half submerged logs. Willows dangled mostly denuded branches into eddies. Each time she stopped, Siao Lin had no difficulty imagining her ancestor walking through such landscapes.

She crossed the river at the first opportunity, near Mannum, and followed a succession of minor roads, arriving in the town of Morgan in the late afternoon.

Siao Lin walked along the banks of the Murray, its thick brown water churning in slanted sunlight. She noticed a faint weedy smell near the water, but it was earthy and not unpleasant. Tamo had passed this way, it was likely this was the last part of the river he saw, for he had followed his new friends into the desert from somewhere nearby. Morgan seemed a pleasant, sleepy little town, with a few tourists wandering aimlessly. She briefly visited the museum, and saw an old paddle wheeler, built around twenty years after her ancestor had passed through.

As she walked along Railway Terrace, she reflected on the antiquity of the buildings and was surprised by the fact that the recorded history of the town was mostly after Tamo had passed through. Even this far south he had been travelling in areas few settlers had arrived in and had met the natives much as they had been for thousands of years. In his diary, Tamo had spoken of them as easy to get along with and very accepting of strangers. She thought back to the strange experiences she'd had in an Adelaide park, and speculated momentarily on what the future would hold for her. She laughed as she spontaneously visualized a mountain of solid gold, shook the vision loose and climbed into her car, started it and took the road to Burra. Seems I have gold fever already, she thought.

The road to Burra crossed flat, arid country. Little else to see but small scrubby bushes interspersed with dusty brown sheep. Ruins were a common sight, and these, with the ever so frequent red clay washouts, showed the harsh nature of the land. The countryside became hillier, with more rocky outcrops nearer to the copper mining town of Burra. At least the road was somewhat improved.

The old mines dominated Burra. Hillsides were scarred and mullock-heap strewn, one huge open cut pit was filled with water. Siao Lin booked into the Burra Motor Inn and ate a meal at Jumbucks Restaurant. She was interested in what she read about the copper mine, which started production some years prior to her ancestor arriving in Australia. She quickly ascertained the mine was essentially a surface deposit, concentrated along a faulted area, through a bed of copper rich meta-sediments. The copper probably had syngenetic origins, being originally concentrated in ocean bottom sediments by the external skeletons of tiny aquatic creatures named diatoms.

The following morning, Siao Lin was on the road before first light, heading north. She passed through a succession of small towns, reaching Yunta around eleven am, where she paid cash to fill her car. There she turned off the main, bituminised road and proceeded northwest on a wide, dusty, dirt road. She constantly thought of Tamo as she drove through the desert. There was no water to be seen from the road at all, save the occasional dam or bore, and none of those would have been around when he had crossed this arid territory. Several times she saw groups of red or grey kangaroos bounding across the bleak landscape. There seemed to be far more dead trees than live ones and the fine red dust soon coated everything inside her vehicle.

Early evening she arrived at Arkaroola village, which turned out to be a privately owned tourist town and wild-life sanctuary. She rented a room for the night, ate a plain dinner and despite the night chill, had a night swim in the pool. After the leisurely swim, she rugged herself up and sat outside with a large glass of fruit juice.

Lights at the front of the reception area shone up and illuminated a nearby ridge of orange quartzite. The rearing, red walls of bare rock made Siao Lin feel at ease, safe in the mountains, and had her looking forward, with a serious yearning, to exploring the area her ancestor had lived in so long ago.

In the morning she asked for information on the state of the dirt tracks she needed to follow and was given accurate advice. She was told that whilst her maps were essentially accurate, finding the right track wasn't always so simple. Often washouts were simply replaced with another section of road and it could be confusing. She cut through on narrow trails for an hour before emerging onto a slightly wider graded road which ran out to Yudnamutana from Copley. Several times she stopped to look at unusual beds of rock, and was especially amazed at the crystalline actinolite which often seemed to sport limonite pseudomorphs of pyrite.

Following the track marked on her map had her trembling with agitation at times, as the vehicle leaned beyond what seemed safe. In places she had to traverse boulder fields where the road was mostly washed away. Despite the rugged nature of the tracks she followed, she was essentially enjoying herself. There were numerous inspiring views, and new valleys would suddenly appear unexpectedly as she drove slowly. The terrain was certainly confusing, mountains became visible quite suddenly and as she drove deeper into the older basement rocks, there seemed very little flat ground between the steep rocky slopes. The final kilometres were covered by driving down a rocky creekbed with towering mountains on all sides. There was no sign of a road, or even wheel-tracks.

At a major creek junction, where an ancient and partly collapsed well had been sunk into the edge of the streambed she drove up the flat left hand bank, onto a stony slope. She turned off the engine and climbed out to find the sky, a fraction of its usual size, diminished by the rocky slopes which soared all around. She soon spied the Wheal Frost copper mine, low on a ridge across the valley, its pale scars a living testament to long dead Welshmen. In a fever of excitement, she followed the small creek upstream and found traces of diggings in the stream bed between two ancient pine trees. They were all gnarled and dead but still standing.

My ancestor dug these pits. Several tears slipped easily across the smooth, tanned skin of her face.

That night, after she had pitched her tent on the slopes above the dry, rocky creekbed, Siao Lin slept a long and dreamless sleep.

17 — Meeting

Siao Lin spent two days exploring the area about her camp. She climbed most of the peaks which ringed the narrow valley. They were mostly barren quartzite with no mineralisation at all. She examined the adits of the Wheal Frost copper mine and found that whilst copper staining was evident, little copper would have been found there. The small amount of copper had mostly been smeared across the hillside near the mine's entrance, enticing and promising, but yielding very little real ore. A few ounces of copper could easily stain a mountainside green.

She had examined the pits dug by Tamo and found that, although they went through the creek sediments, down into the weathered actinolitic marble below, no gold would ever have come from them. The environment was wrong, the gold must have come from somewhere else altogether.

She lay back on her sleeping bag and looked at the worn cover of Tamo's old diary. The faded red cover was cracked with shrinkage. She opened it and began to read.

August, 1857
I was well clear of the town before daylight forced me to move into the high sandhills which flanked the beach. Behind the sandhills was a narrow freshwater marsh. It appeared the beach I walked was remote and unreachable except along its length. I decided to push on during daylight hours.

I followed the beach for four days, living mostly on small but tasty sand clams. I even caught the occasional fish in the crashing waves of the seashore. These I cooked over smokeless fires after darkness fell, in the shelter of the sand hills. I saw no sign of habitation, nor any people; I was literally in a world of my own.

On the fourth day I saw several, near naked, dark skinned men. I took them to be natives of the country. They were collecting clams ahead of me on the beach. I remained unseen and they soon vanished into the sand hills.

On the morning of my fifth day on the long beach, I came to a large river. Muddy brown water pushed lazily into the ocean. Several small boats stood out to sea. Numerous thin plumes of smoke rose into the still air someway ahead. I turned inland, away from civilisation, and was forced to wade the wide but shallow swamp, and follow the course of the river.

The following day, just before sunset, I met a group of about twenty natives. I watched them catch a large speckled fish by stretching a hand woven net across a hollow log lodged against the river bank. They moved easily in the water, one holding a net and a second pounding on the far end of the log with a stone. The huge fish rushed out into the net and was soon hoisted ashore.

I called to them as they emerged from the water with the fish.

Several of the men spoke to me in their own language. They dropped the flapping fish onto the riverbank and flocked about me. Several held spears and stones. They spoke no words I could fathom, nor could I speak to them.

I waved my knife about and mimicked handing it to the tallest warrior, the one who had netted the fish. I drew the knife back as the man tried to take it.

This amused everyone in the group, save the tall man who had caught the fish. He grabbed a spear from one of the others, his eyes never leaving my knife. The others stepped away, forming a rough circle about us. I lay the knife on the ground with my bundle and adopted a defensive posture.

The man jabbed the spear toward me. It wasn't quite going to reach me, I didn't move. Again the tall aborigine feinted with the spear. I beckoned the man to come forward. He lunged quickly with the spear, straight at my stomach. I stepped aside and took the spear from his extended grasp with a subtle jerk. I plunged the spear deeply into the ground, picked up my knife and walked to the fish. I gestured at the fish and my stomach. I pointed at the tall man and then to my knife.

The aborigine grinned and laughed, his teeth bright in the fading light. He stepped forward. I gave him the knife and took the fish up.

Twenty dark men watched me strike a fire with my flint and steel. There was much talk and nodding amongst the onlookers.

We cooked the fish by sitting it in the coals of the large fire. If some was burned and some raw, none of us minded. That night I not only earned respect but apparently a name. They called me literally quickfire. I sat at ease by that fire; the charred fish filled my belly. There was much talk and I watched and listened intently.

Even the first night I learned many of their words, including those for fish and spear. That wasn't surprising, for as well as learning the Shaolin style of self-defence and attack, I had been trained to learn new languages quickly.

I travelled with them for several days up the river before a small village near a sharp bend of the river barred the way. The aborigines wouldn't follow the river further.

Most of the group simply turned and walked back along the muddy brown river to the south, whilst the half dozen men remaining, pointed animatedly to the Northwest, indicating I travel with them.

The fires I lit so easily pleased them. Shortly after we left the river they speared a heavy animal which travelled by means of long hopping leaps. I'd seen several similar, but had never been close enough to attempt to kill one.

They danced on through the night, painting themselves and burying the animal in the earth beneath a large fire, removing it to eat the half burned, half raw meat in the early hours of the morning.

The moon went from full to no moon whilst we travelled. Water was not found every day and it was no use my carrying it in my bags, for the group drank it within a few hours. Doubtless, I would have died of thirst in crossing this dry land without their knowledge. They always knew where water lay.

On rising one morning I was surprised to see a high range of mountains ahead. They rose stark and bare, contrasting the red sandhills and small dry lakebeds we had crossed. Orange rock faces shone bright in the early morning sunshine. I could by that time speak some of their words and nearly make myself understood. My name remained Quickfire.

Where the desert plain met the steep mountains we met a large group of natives by a long, deep pool they called Paralana. Precipitous cliffs ranged around three sides. An out-welling of water was near boiling and we lay in it to relax our weary muscles.

The next day we walked a little to the south to where a major creekbed cut through the mountains. We walked upstream a short way to where several caves perched above a steep bend in the river. The caves were an important holy site for the men of the tribe. I always thought of these caves as eyes, the caves of the eyes.

Siao Lin put the diary down and gazed out through the flyscreen of the tent. The night beyond her flickering tilly-lamp was black. A few large insects bounced off the nylon fabric. She turned off the lamp and sank down into her bedding. Sleep claimed her quickly, thoughts of Tamo drifting into dreams of a giant straddling the mountains. The mile high giant was laughing as he tore huge chunks of stone from the mountain tops and threw them about. Suddenly the giant was aware of her sleeping below. Siao Lin was terrified! She felt his gaze catch her as his laughter rumbled like thunder. If he was Benign, he was incredibly fearsome.

18 — A Leaky Boat

The day after I got back to Adelaide, I went in to the office early. No point trying to track the girl, she'd lost us and would almost certainly turn up in the long run. At that stage I was more concerned about our security leak.

Dave called me over and introduced me to one of our IT sleuths; I'd actually been close to the mark with my accusations, at least so far as Bill was concerned. His home computer had been compromised and we'd never have known if the virus hadn't tried to infiltrate our own network. The hacker was savvy; he wrote good code, but not that good. They'd traced him already. We'd probably recruit him eventually.

Dave finished by telling me Bill's censure was in my court and he'd back whatever decision I made. Within seconds, wouldn't you believe it, Bill wandered in.

I walked straight up to him, blocking his path. Privacy wasn't an issue, you did something in this office and you wore the rewards.

'You got a problem Bill,' I said.

He glared at me, waiting for me to continue, the fact that Dave was sitting at his desk, simply watching, sank in immediately. Couldn't call him slow.

'This gold thing is compromised,' I got right to the issue. 'Dominick has had access to everything you have.'

'Look Russ,' Bill was adamant. 'I gave almost nothing to Dominick. I only spoke to him on the phone once. An' yeh, before you ask, I told him you were a loose cannon. If that was wrong, it was not in what I said, but who I said it to.'

'Remember that email he sent you,' I said, as evenly as my building temper would allow. I wanted to hit him a couple of times.

Bill nodded, obviously still defiant. I poked him good and hard in the chest with a finger, knowing he'd take it, but kinda' wishing he'd swing on me.

'That link to his site,' I continued, shaking my head. 'Clicking it allowed a really mean little key-logger into your computer. Almost got into our system.'

His head dropped a fraction and his eyes left mine. He hadn't known at all. Guess that was one plus. He was a bloody good agent actually, hating me had clouded his judgement. I could understand his hate; didn't I hate myself half the time. Not an excuse at all, but probably enough of a reason to keep him on.

I walked away from him, nodding to Dave with a bit of a grimace as I passed his desk on the way out. He could placate Bill; it was his fault really for letting it go so far. I knew Bill would want to go and settle up with Dominick and that could only end badly either way. Guys like Dominick always got what they deserve in the end, best let his own kind sort him out.

Nothing on the girl the next day either. Dave phoned and told me to call in later, whenever I felt like it. Bill was there when I turned up in the afternoon. He looked at me once, then looked away. Back to his old quiet and moody self.

Dave told me that Bill had actually asked if he could head up to Coffs and sort Dominick out.

'Reckon we should keep him on?' Dave sounded very reluctant when it came to sacking him.

'Good question Dave,' I replied, nodding but keeping the smile I felt from appearing. I let a few seconds pass before continuing.

'He'll be alright,' I conceded. 'Be right on the ball now.'

'You alright with that Russ?'

'Yeh, 'course. What are you gonna' do about Dominick though?'

'Keep feedin' him,' Dave was smiling.

'Anything particular in mind?'

'Seems Dominick's hacker has been keeping tabs on the AMDEL site too. That place is full of leaks, those lads sell everything to the highest bidder it seems. Be a good way to slip some bogus info through for now.'

Dave went on to tell me we'd traced two bank deposits from Dominick's account. May not have been related, but Zihnjihn, a large Chinese mining organisation, had a slush fund which fed their dirty tricks branch. Two withdrawals of cash had been made shortly before Dominic's deposits. The first was for a different amount, but Dominick had hired some lads too, so the Chinese could well be using Dominick as a front for investigating Siao Lin. He asked if I had any ideas.

I admitted I hadn't anything firm, just that I agreed with the notion that Dominick still saw Bill as a potential site for information.

Dave had the notion of getting something incriminating on the Chinese. I was a bit dubious. He had notions of entrapping them, setting up the girl as bait, using the cobalt riddled gold as a shiny lure for a real big fish.

When he'd finished speaking, I told him I thought we had no time for elaborate ruses. We simply needed to make sure that when the girl surfaced, they didn't know about it. I didn't see the point in making things more complicated, we knew where the bad guys were; close by we could watch them easier. If we lost them, we needed to be sure they didn't get the jump on us, but I just couldn't see the point in pussy footing around.

'How can she just up and disappear?' asked Dave. 'Surely she should have made a slip by now?'

'She's gone bush somewhere,' I told him what I thought, after all it seemed obvious to me. 'Maybe looking for the gold at the same time. We need to tie up with her once she re-appears. She didn't want to know me when I met her, just have to convince her somehow.'

'I spoke to Harry at AMDEL,' added Dave, sidetracking. 'They've given up on the samples, not enough country rock for them to identify any sort of accurate location and the gold's telluride balance indicates it's from a deposit not on their database.'

As I left the office, I thought on the whole leaky boat thing. Dave's idea of leading Dominic on a wild goose chase was all and well in theory, but I wasn't completely sure we'd plugged all the leaks. Reckoned from then on that I'd keep my own council so far as Siao Lin was concerned, that was, if we ever located her again. I already had enough respect for her to not want to see her come to any harm; at least I think it was respect.

I noticed as Bill left for the evening, he hardly glanced my way. I wondered how I could get it through to him that I didn't hate him. I didn't even think badly about his latest slip up; what had happened between him and Dominick could have happened to me just as easily. I knew he'd bounce back too, how could he go on hating me just 'cause I saved his life. I thought about visiting Una, really meant to too, couple of close by pubs put paid to that though.

19 — Gold & Poppies

On the third morning after arriving in the Wheal Frost valley, Siao Lin set out down the stream bed of the Yudnamutana Creek. She carried water, dried fruit and some salty biscuits, as well as a bedroll. As she walked down the boulder strewn streambed, the slopes to her left were nearly vertical, looking too steep to climb, rising up five hundred metres at least. The creekbed itself was a jumble of boulders, sand and pebbles, scattered at varying levels, often soft and awkward to walk on.

She quickly spotted the distinctive purple flowers of small opium poppies, which grew on many of the raised banks along the side of the dry streambed. Tamo must have planted their ancestors.

She referred to the map fifteen minutes later, as another similar sized tributary entered the streambed from the north. It was the Daly Mine Creek, apparently there were several copper mines along the ridges which overlooked it. Something else to visit when time allowed.

China had plenty of mountainous country, and Siao Lin had seen much of it, yet the amount of bare rock exposed along the Yudnamutana creek was breathtaking. On both sides, vertical walls of quartzite allowed only a thirty metre space for the river bed. It was, however, anything but straight; the looping of deeply incised meanders told Siao Lin that the streambed had cut down through the mountains as they'd risen about it, leaving it to still follow the meandering course it had laid down when the terrain had been relatively flat.

After an hour's further walking, the mountains eventually relented and began to crowd in less. They were still steep and craggy, but nearer 45 degrees than 90. The river course still meandered, but the curves were not as deeply incised. At a place where the river turned sharply, Siao Lin noticed a large outcropping of breccia. Several high caves looked out over the streambed, like the eyes of an ancient carving of a god. This must be the cave of the eyes which Tamo referred to, she thought, remembering his relevant diary entry, *I must be nearly though the mountains.*

She was soon proven correct; the mountains were behind her,

the creekbed fanned out. She walked up the slope to the left of the creek, pushing through thick, pale green stands of juvenile river red gums. After a short walk across two intervening ridges she arrived at the Paralana Hot Springs, where Tamo had lived for much of his life.

They seemed narrower and shallower than he had described, perhaps silted up by flooding. The surface of the steaming water was clothed in a thick mat of weedy algae. She parted the smelly stuff, which was up to 15 centimetres thick, and saw clear steaming water and a coarse sandy bottom.

She initially tried to enter the water near the upstream end of the pool, but discovered it was too hot. Five metres downstream the temperature was more to her liking. As she eased her tired body into the waters, she first thought they were still a little too hot, but was soon able to relax. Siao Lin closed her eyes and enjoyed a dreamy feeling of utter relaxation. The hot waters soothed her aching muscles and she breathed deeply and let all her worries vanish.

Ten or fifteen minutes later she reached to her pack and took out the diary Tamo had written. She leaned back on the smooth stone at the edge of the waters and leafed through it, her body and legs still immersed in the hot springs.

December, 1875

My new home was a harsh place. The simplicity and strength of those I shared it with was most satisfying and tempered the adverse conditions; making it bearable. Never once was I spurned as an outsider, I was simply from elsewhere and seemed to be a welcome addition to their tribe. The longer I remained, the more at ease I became with their lifestyle and within a year I had a young and handsome wife; and soon thereafter, a young and handsome child.

I saw many things over the years, was basically happy, yet felt a looming sadness for the people I had become a part of. I laughed with my friends at explorers who arrived with a whaleboat, presumably to cross an inland sea which didn't exist. Pastoralists took the land as their own, ignoring those who had always lived there. Tribal ways were changing, as many of the prime places were occupied by settlers. My new people bend with the winds of change, accepting these changes as they would a flood or a drought, or even the influx of a much stronger tribe from the north. Miners stripped the valleys of their copper, then vanished again, leaving the scars of mines and smelters behind.

March, 1898

Most of the tribe have moved south and live on one of the cattle and sheep stations. I discovered gold further north and baked some into the clay of hollow statues I made. I will send them by mail to China in a parcel containing these notes I have made on my life. North from Paralana, just past the third small creek there is a soak. Nearby, amongst the circles carved by my tribe as they waited for lizards to emerge from rocky cracks, I have carved my rune and buried the rest.

I alone remain at Paralana. My heart is in these mountains. I grew some poppies and smoke the opium to ease my pain. They thrive along the dry riverbed which cuts right through the mountains.

I found a large jar of honey left behind by some miners. It was sweet and delicious. I remember my youth. Travelling in the hills, and seeking honey from huge bee colonies in limestone caves. I think of my grandchildren, in the desert. I drift with the opium, and laugh with the Giant who made the mountains. He is far older than the snake who carved the meandering river and much easier to talk to too.

I feel the pleasant warmth of the sand beneath me, as faint wisps of steam drift across my fading vision.

Siao Lin re-read what Tamo had written about carving a rune. What had he left there? Could it be more gold? There could be several meanings, but she must find the place and investigate.

She moved herself across the shallow pool, parting the thick algae as she moved downstream. The water became a little cooler and she found herself better able to relax there. Her eyes gazed, only partly focussed, on a thick growth of young gum trees further down the streambed. Her eyes closed and she felt sleep closing in. The warm waters soothed her further and she breathed deeply and let all her worries vanish.

She studied the white trunk of a huge and ancient gum tree, leaves swept across the upper portion in a fitful breeze. She saw the same young aboriginal man she had seen before. He laughed at her distress and confusion and drew several characters in the sand. She read them, for they were Chinese characters. They mentioned an area of granite north of the out-welling of the hot-springs.

The youth laughed and mentioned that all about she would see circles carved over the centuries whilst men waited for lizards to emerge from the cracks in the rocks. Nearby, the granite bore Chinese pictograms, a message carved by her ancestor. Before Siao Lin could read the words, the youth began to tell her of a story he had learned in his younger days, a story he claimed she would need to find her way.

She awoke suddenly, startled, as a magpie two meters away began singing to her. She remembered her dream and how in it she had heard the story of the giant snake Arkaroo and of his eternal wanderings through the mountain home of the Adnyamathanha people. Then she remembered the youth and what he'd said. It certainly tied in with what she'd read in the diary; perhaps that was why she'd dreamed such a dream.

But it was so clear, Siao Lin thought as she dressed, remembering the clarity of her latest vision. Shaking her head with a shiver, she cleared her mind and set off northward, along the edges of the area of mountains known as the Freeling Heights. Half an hour later she came across a plain where granite was outcropping and flat, dome-like areas were exposed. On most of the relatively smooth surfaces circles had been carved, most were small at 10cm to 15cm, but a few were larger and all were deeply inscribed. After a little looking she found some Chinese characters, as she'd been led to expect. She laughed at the message.

No lizards here now, walk ten metres east, under a large boulder, dig to locate what is hidden.

The boulder, hopefully it was the right one, she thought, was way too heavy for her to lift, but Siao Lin managed to dig under it and roll it to one side. As she began digging down, a very big black and yellow lizard scampered from nearby bushes to its refuge in a large exfoliation crack in the granite. She nodded as she remembered the story the aboriginal youth had told her about the carvings and how they were made by men waiting for lizards to emerge.

Ten minutes later she struck a solid object which turned out to be a crudely fired clay jar. It took another 45 minutes to dig it out, as it was too heavy to lift. She certainly didn't want to break it. It was a direct link to her ancestor and hence deserving of care and reverence. She would treasure it, even as she sold the gold which she suspected was to be found within. She eventually cleared enough dirt and stony rubble to remove the lid, and then take out the heavy nuggets of gold to allow her to lift the pot free. She turned it over and found on the bottom the pot maker's name; Tamo. As she saw his mark Siao Lin felt like doing a little dance. Instead she simply grinned, put the pot down carefully and looked to the large pile of gold.

She examined the gold carefully, using her geologist's eyes and quickly noticed with interest that some of the pieces had bedrock attacked. Siao Lin grinned even more, looking at the black, basic, fine to medium grained rock. This may well show me where it came from, she thought, grinning in anticipation, and I never thought to bring a microscope. She hefted one of the larger solid pieces of yellow metal and estimated it to be around half a kilo. The twenty pieces she had removed from the jar would weigh at least ten kilos. Numbers ticked over in her mind. Her rudimentary calculation came to $350,000 at least. I can buy a house in NSW, she thought, feeling the lure of gold fever raising her feeling of excitement.

She replaced a bit more than half the gold back in the hole, re-filling it and removing all trace of her being there. She carried the pot and gold back to the hotsprings in her backpack, and it was certainly heavy. Sweaty and tired out from having dug a very large hole and filling it in again, not to mention hauling an additional five or six kilos, she enjoyed the soothing waters of the hot springs for the second time that day. The restorative properties of the waters were remarkable, and she had quickly become used to the strong smell of the thick algal mats, barely noticing it at all.

As the sun vanished behind the looming Freeling Plateau to the east, Siao Lin decided to make the long walk back to camp. She did make it by dark, barely, but it was a far longer walk than she expected, being uphill and with her carrying such a heavy load. If she had any dreams that night she didn't remember them at all.

20 — Southward

After further exploration around the Wheal Frost area, it was obvious to Siao Lin the gold wasn't from anywhere nearby. It also couldn't have been from where she'd found the large stash of gold, her ancestor had hidden, the un-mineralised granite was barren.

She had little to help her locate the gold's source; there was only the dark bedrock, attached to some of the pieces of gold, to guide her. To pursue this line of identification, she'd need a good microscope to examine the samples properly. Then she'd have to spend time searching for similar beds of rock, and run comparisons, until she found a match.

She wandered about for two full days after her return from Paralana Hotsprings, all the time thinking of how she could locate the source, but deep down knowing she would need a lab. She took her mind off worrying by investigating the Daly Mine area, quickly deciding the Adelaidean metasediments would never yield gold such as her ancestor had found. She climbed to the top of Commonwealth Hill and enjoyed a view out across the plains to the east and the white salt lakes of Frome and the more distant Callabonna. The basement area between Mt Painter and the granite dome of the Armchair appeared interesting, piquing her geological investigative nature; she decided to have a better look when she could find the time.

The spinifex was so thick on her return trip, it spiked her badly. She had also been frightened and had a narrow escape when a whole scree slope she was traversing, began to avalanche down, as she stood on it. Her ankle had been caught between moving boulders and badly bruised. Eventually she managed to hobble off that treacherous talus debris. As she limped along the creekbed, back to her camp, she began to view the mountains with a lot more respect. They were grand and beautiful, but there were certainly dangers; dangers which she now knew could spring out of no-where.

Even before her injury, she'd already come to the conclusion she would have to return to Adelaide and make use of a good microscope to examine slides of the dark bedrock attached to the gold. She decided to stake a claim somewhere, so she could cash in the gold legally. It was too much to carry about with her for long and she couldn't bear to hide it again. It didn't take her long to decide where to hammer her pegs in.

After staking the claim near the Wheal Frost, in the creekbed where Tamo had dug his two pits, Siao Lin packed her Toyota and drove westward, opting to drive out through Copley, rather than try and find her way back through Arkaroola and then take the long, flat country trip to Yunta. Despite a chilly morning start, the steady sun soon warmed the day. Before she reached Copley, in the afternoon, it became quite hot in the cabin of the Landcruiser. Hot and dusty; seemed everything was dusty in that part of the world. The trip was very shaky from the relentless shuddering as the car bounded over corrugations in the poorly maintained dirt surface, not doing her ankle much good at all. She made a mental note to make her next trip through Yunta, also a long, dusty trip, but with a better maintained road surface.

Siao Lin had a long break in the small town of Copley, where she took a most welcome, if slightly salty, shower in the caravan park. Afterward, she sat and sipped a rather bland cup of coffee, in no real hurry to hit the road again. She smiled as she watched the antics of the pink and grey galahs screeching and squawking in the wide yard, car park area, in front of the shop.

Eventually she headed south, in the early afternoon, with the sun on her right and red quartzite mountains on her left. Kangaroos continually crossed from either side, at times causing her to brake and swerve, but she somehow managed to miss them all. Just before dark she reached the town of Hawker, and booked into the hotel for the night. She ate an overcooked meal of battered fish and soggy vegetables in a large room where three tired and dusty looking cowboys propped up the well-worn bar.

Leaving early in the morning, she was glad to be back on sealed roads again, by-passing Quorn and Pt. Augusta before stopping at Pt. Germaine for a counter lunch at the hotel there. She started to walk along the weedy seafront, despite the tide being out and the water half a kilometre away, but her ankle was too sore. She took her boot off carefully. It was swollen and dark with bruising and she decided to get someone to look at it.

As she drove out of Pt. Germaine, Siao Lin decided to stop at the next large town and have her injury looked at. She drove south with the shallow sea of the Spencer Gulf off to her right and the striking, blocky scarps of the southernmost Flinders Ranges on her left. Turning off the main Adelaide Road, she drove around until she located the hospital at Pt. Pirie. As she limped in to the casualty section, she noted with interest that two flags flew at the front. One was Australian and the other was the Aboriginal flag.

She was wondering how she could get treatment without having to use her real name and had just about decided she would have to give in and use it anyway, when a nurse came out to take her details. The girl was Chinese and after an initial greeting even spoke to her in Mandarin. Her name was Mai Ling Down.

Siao Lin gave her name and told the girl of her ankle and how she thought she would need some drugs for both the pain and the swelling.

Mai Ling appeared to sense Siao Lin's reluctance to leave a record of her being there. She had a quick look at the ankle and told Siao Lin she would be taking a lunch break in a few minutes and that she could attend to her at her own home, which was not far away.

Siao Lin nodded, relieved, and said she would wait in her car outside, the dusty Toyota Landcruiser.

Mai Ling soon came out and drove with Siao Lin to her flat where she soaked the ankle, bent and poked it awhile before pronouncing it just badly bruised, not broken. She rubbed it with a mixture of liniment and local anaesthetic, and bandaged it tightly. She gave Siao Lin some drugs to reduce the swelling, and others for the pain. Siao Lin offered to pay Mai Ling, but the girl refused to accept payment, saying one day she could return the favour. She asked if Siao Lin needed further help, mentioning that her father was head of an Australian-Chinese organisation for ex-Chinese nationals living in the country.

Siao Lin took Mai's mobile number and promised to call her. She dropped her off at the hospital. They hugged with affection as they parted and Siao Lin had a strange feeling of familiarity with the girl. She decided she would indeed contact Mai Ling again, and soon, for true friendships were rare enough in these modern times; especially so when one was in a foreign land.

An hour and a half after leaving Pt. Pirie, Siao Lin arrived in the town of Pt. Wakefield. The sun was setting, it would be too late to call in to the Department of Mines that day, so Siao Lin decided to stay at an old hotel named the Rising Sun, and venture on to Adelaide in the morning.

The Rising Sun Hotel was interesting, as it had numerous old pictures and documents relating to the history of the town, all about its walls. Siao Lin enjoyed the fresh grilled fish and salad she ordered and slept deeply, possibly due to the heavy dose of pain killers Mai Ling had given her.

In the morning, she found her ankle much improved, the swelling was considerably less; it was still sore and bruised, but with care, she could walk on it easily enough. The morning was bright and sunny, and she ate a quick breakfast of eggs and toast and set out for Adelaide, a hundred kilometres to the south.

21 — Back into the mix

On her arrival in Adelaide, Siao Lin headed straight for the Department of mines. She introduced herself, checked leases in the area and was relieved she could claim the area she had pegged out. More importantly, she noticed a large swath of land along the east of the mountains for twenty miles north of Paralana was under no lease at all. That was the area she would expect the gold to have been found. She registered the claim in her own name, also purchasing some plans which showed all the present leases in the area. She collected some more detailed geological maps of the area. All in all she spent about an hour there.

She left the building, half thinking about booking into the same hotel she'd used previously, but also wondering whether that was such a good idea. As she walked through a screening of native plants in stone lined planter beds, she saw a figure ahead. She looked up automatically and got a hell of a shock. There, standing as if expecting her, was Peter Millar. She had to walk right by him as he was waiting at the entrance to the car park. He seemed alone, she fingered her keys nervously, it couldn't be coincidence; he'd obviously been waiting for her.

'What do you want Peter?' she asked as civilly as she could.

'Hi Siao Lin,' Peter smiled faintly. 'I may as well get straight to the point; it's about the gold that was stolen from you at Coffs Harbour.'

Siao Lin let him go on.

'Bottom line is it's high in cobalt. The government is very interested in it and where it came from.'

'Are you working for the government now?' asked Siao Lin, knowing full well he wasn't.

Peter half nodded.

'What do you know about the break in to my room?' she asked, watching him closely.

'I heard about it from the Park Beach Hotel,' he said after a pause. 'Some of the gold that was taken surfaced in Victoria, was analysed and found to be high in cobalt. That's when I was contacted about it.'

'Why didn't you tell me then?' she asked.

'They wanted me to ask you where it came from, I thought you'd react badly. I should have…'

'Just leave me alone,' Siao Lin cut him off, but kept her voice even despite the agitation she was feeling. 'I don't believe you, I don't trust you Peter. Just leave me alone.'

Peter was nonplussed and seemed to be trying to find something to say.

She walked by him and headed for her Toyota.

'Siao Lin,' he called, following after her. 'This is important, for your own good you need to co-operate.'

Siao Lin turned as she opened the car door.

'At least I prefer threats to subterfuge Peter,' she made no attempt to hide her disdain for the man she had once regarded as a good friend.

She started the engine.

Peter was forced to jump back as she reversed

'Those men who attacked you on the rig are looking for you,' he called as she selected first gear. 'You need protection.'

She drove out of the car-park and quickly into the wide traffic clogged stretch of South Terrace. She stopped at a red light before she realised she was shaking. Confronting Peter had almost paralysed her. And yet I did what I wanted, she thought, forcing her body to relax. It was easy; she had been trained to relax. I have been as assertive as necessary. I know that in the future I'll be able to do it again. The lights changed and she followed the traffic around to the right.

Russell came to mind. Even though they'd only met once, and that briefly, she remembered feeling trust. I felt he was rough but trustworthy, she thought. She drove her car to the top of the Central Market car-park, took her backpack out and hefted it onto her shoulders. The gold was inside, it was very heavy. She walked through bustling city streets, looked in a few shops, but all the while thought over what she should do next. Eventually she gave in to the notion she felt was right. At a payphone on Rundle Mall, Siao Lin called the number on the card Russell had given her.

'Hi Russell,' she found herself smiling as she spoke. 'This is Siao Lin.'

His reply mirrored his surprise.

'I'm back in Adelaide, quite close to where we last met,' she continued.

'What do I want,' she repeated his question. 'I want to see you, concerning some more of that gold you were so interested in. Thought I'd give you first option on it.'

He agreed to meet her in an hour, at the same park bench they'd met at previously. With an hour to spend, Siao Lin walked up to the city and along Rundle Mall, feeling relatively safe in the bustling street. Part of the reason she'd called Russell was to have it out; to get beyond whatever schemes and machinations were going on, disarm them and be able to lighten up.

She walked out of the city and into the parkland. Oddly enough, the same youth was sitting on the grass, playing guitar and singing. It wasn't the same song, but it was slow and ethereal. Siao Lin felt it lulling her, even as she walked by. She sat on the grass a little away from the youth and listened. The arpeggios were soft and harmonious, but the initial words raw.

'Just lie and grasp the glimpses of your dream,
touch fingers on their dewy morning blades,
grass growing to the sun,
flying in the sunrise just before the wind is born,
before the sunlight creeps across the land in shadow still
and calm beneath the sky.'

She felt herself drifting, and was certainly tired after several days travelling. Shouldn't fall asleep, she thought. She tried to open her eyes, they seemed stuck shut. Her vision came into focus; Siao Lin was back in the mountains. There was familiarity in the scene there hadn't been the previous time. She smiled at the raucous cry of two cockatoos as they swooped out of an old river red gum. This was country she knew now. Birds she understood.

The aboriginal youth she had seen previously was abruptly in front of her as the dream strengthened.

'Am I asleep?'

She saw the trees had red auras. The song continued, ever so slowly.

'Does it matter,' replied the dark skinned youth, smiling.

'You think you've found it,' he said, his tone more sober, losing the grin. 'You haven't.'

Siao Lin knew he was right. She needed to find the source of the gold.

'Not just that,' replied the boy, had he read her thoughts. 'You need to find me, and your ancestor, and yourself. You've chosen a hard road, but you can't turn around, it's a one way street.'

He laughed again. As Siao Lin smiled, his laughter echoed and dissolved into the song which continued to its climax. She knew she'd never heard that song before but it seemed so familiar.

Again her eyes opened, the real world. Which was the real world? What she saw had her taking a deep breath and holding it. The view was anything but mundane. The few trees still clothed seemed bright, even the colour of the grass had a clarity which made her smile. The youth who'd been playing stopped, having finished the song, placed his guitar into its case, stood up and walked away, further into the parkland. She thought to follow and thank him for his song, but as she stood, remembered her rendezvous with Russell, on the other side of the city.

The second park experience had amazed her as much as the first, for it gave a seeming reality and solidity to what had probably been an imaginary occurrence the previous time. She realised that the images were real in a sense. Somewhere, somehow, she felt Tamo had asked her to trust in what was happening.

Russell was waiting on the bench where they'd met previously. He looked like he hadn't had a lot of sleep lately.

'Sorry I'm late,' she began, sitting beside him, leaving a metre or so between them.

Siao Lin watched as a mother duck quacked its way along the edge of the Torrens Lake, a tribe of tiny ducklings running in its wake. She flapped into the water, her fuzzy progeny following happily.

'Have you been here long?' she asked.

'About half an hour,' he admitted. 'Don't worry about it.'

'I'll get right to the point. Just who is actually chasing me?' she asked.

'Don't know exactly,' he admitted. 'There's an ex-mercenary named Frank and the driller who attacked you on the rig. We think Zihnjihn may be funding that group, but they may also have their own personnel on it too. Other than that I don't know, probably several other mining companies are interested too.

'I left the mines department this morning, after filing a claim. My old chief geologist, from Exminoil, was waiting outside for me. I brushed him off, but that was what prompted me to call you.'

Russell mentioned he'd met Millar and found him harmless enough.

'Will you buy the gold off me?' she asked.

'We will,' he agreed. 'We'll give you whatever the market price is. How much do you have?'

'About five kilos,' she smiled. 'There's at least that much more buried where I got this. My ancestor hid it; I still don't know where it came from though.'

He asked where the gold was and Siao Lin hefted her backpack from the ground and swung it to him.

'Feels more like ten or fifteen kilos,' he said laughing as he weighed the bag in his hands.

'Could well be,' Siao Lin nodded, returning his smile. 'It's getting heavier and heavier the more I walk around with it.'

22 – Unlikely Partnership

Siao Lin called me, totally out of the blue. It was in the morning, a week and a half after we'd lost track of her. I'd just arrived at Una's place. Why was I there? Bit of a story; I'd gotten pretty drunk the night I got back from chasing that crazy Chinese girl and woke up on the sofa in Una's lounge. After nearly a week of deliberating, I'd gotten up early and decided to visit her and thank her for dragging me home. I'd been there all of ten minutes when the call came.

I agreed to meet Siao Lin in an hour, at the place we met before, by the Torrens. She sounded a bit rattled on the phone. Una brought coffee in and sat down opposite.

'You gotta' go eh.' She was bloody sharp that girl.

I stayed for five minutes and finished the coffee. It was just how I like it, strong and black.

I arrived at the arranged meeting place right on time, which was half an hour before Siao Lin turned up. I was starting to wonder by the time she showed. She apologised for being late and then asked who was actually chasing her. I had to admit to some uncertainty, I didn't know exactly. I told her about Frank and one of the drillers who'd attacked her on the rig.

'Just the one?' she asked, as if she was expecting to hear about them.

I told her I'd put one out of action whilst off looking for her.

'Who else?' she asked.

I mentioned that several mining companies were interested in the high cobalt readings, and a large Chinese company named Zihnjihn was more than likely funding Frank and whoever was working with him.

She told me about meeting her old chief geologist, from Exminoil, in the car park of the Department of Mines, and admitted that was what prompted her to call me. They'd found her so quickly she had suddenly realised she was in a bit of trouble. She also added she'd rather not talk to him, she couldn't trust him. He'd somehow gained knowledge about her stolen gold, when she had never told anyone that gold had been stolen. She admitted that was the reason she'd fled down to Adelaide.

I mentioned that I'd met Peter Millar and thought he was pretty harmless and not in any sort of loop which would actually threaten her. Exminoil were interested, but they didn't have any undercover personnel. Then I had a thought that I was amazed had not arisen earlier.

'Did you just tell me that you overheard Millar talking about your gold before you left Coffs Harbour? Was it the day before?'

Siao Lin nodded. 'Yes, the day before. As I said, it was what prompted me to leave so suddenly.'

'Then he knew before we did.' I was speaking as I thought. 'I'd better have another talk with him.'

Siao Lin interrupted my musing and asked if I would buy the gold and I said we would pay her market price for it, asking how much she had. She said she had at least five kilos. I asked where it was and she handed me a backpack. I hefted it and could feel there was more like fifteen kilos in it; she'd been wandering around the city with a fortune in gold in her backpack.

I asked her to come for lunch and we could discuss what we were going to do next. I laughed and told her she'd done a good job of disappearing, but mentioned it would get harder and harder to stay lost.

We walked to the Cayenne, which I'd kept using in case I needed to suddenly head off. It was nearby and I drove us down to Glenelg. We ate upstairs in a place I know is cool.

'So this gold was left by your great great grandfather?' I asked once we'd ordered.

'Yes,' she agreed. 'As I mentioned earlier, I don't know where it came from yet. I've pegged a claim already, but it's not where the gold is from.'

That was definitely something she shouldn't have done at this stage.

'You mentioned that earlier,' I said. 'I was hoping you meant you were thinking of doing it. That claim will attract lots of people; some of them might be pretty bad.'

'I never thought of it that way until after I'd registered,' she admitted. 'As I said, the claim isn't anywhere near where the gold comes from. They won't be any the wiser and it will bring them out in the open.'

'There are some of them who would kill you!'

'I didn't know that until just now.' She was obviously feeling well out of her depth again and looked frightened. 'Will you look after me then?'

I said I would, of course, and didn't admit to Siao Lin that her registering the claim worried me a lot. I finished my beer and reached under the table, dragging out the backpack, opening it and looking in. It was full of gold alright. I again thought about her walking around the town with close to three quarters of a million in gold on her back. I told her I'd find a more secure place for her to stay this time, not mentioning what I had in mind.

Siao Lin nodded.

I told her there were a lot of players in the game, almost definitely some we didn't know about. We knew some were on the dangerous side, but to what lengths they were prepared to go, we had no real idea. I asked for her car keys, to have her car moved somewhere safe and she handed them to me without questioning it. I added I could arrange to pay her for the gold, whenever she wanted the money. I told her I'd feel a lot safer if I was the only one to know where she was. She simply nodded again, it was kinda' good to feel trusted.

'Peter told me today that lots of heavy people were around and looking for me,' she said.

'That's why you called me?' I asked, nodding.

'I guess that was the final straw,' she agreed, her turn to nod.

'Lesser of two evils eh,' I had to grin.

'My thoughts exactly,' Siao Lin returned my smile.

'So you've no idea where the gold came from?' I asked, restarting the conversation after we'd finished our main course.

She shook her head. 'Not really. I haven't any real idea where the gold could have come from yet.'

'Is it somewhere near where you got the gold from?

'I would think so,' she replied. 'My great grandfather's diary doesn't mention where the gold came from at all.'

I asked her if she intended to locate the source of the gold. She said she did, but that she'd need some equipment. I asked what sort of equipment, she told me she'd have to have a good microscope and a diamond saw to cut paper-thin slides.

I suggested we pay a visit to AMDEL, they were the people who detected the cobalt in the gold initially.

She nodded. I didn't tell her that going to AMDEL was a little risky; it was in no way secure. Nor did I mention I'd decided to keep her out of the government loop for the time being, still unsure whether our security remained compromised. I had to assume, that in spite of our best efforts, it was.

'Once I've cut the slides and examined them, I will need to match my results with rocks from the area. Not sure yet how difficult that will be, I'll have a better look at the geological maps once we've examined the samples. I might need to have the bedrock dated too.'

She seemed a bit worried, but certainly less so than when I'd met first her. She seemed to trust me and I felt I could trust her too. I just hoped to hell I wouldn't let her down. Too many unknowns, I really had no idea what I was up against.

We did a bit of a transport shuffle, just in case. Took the tram from Glenelg to Adelaide, where I called Dave on his mobile. Got him at home, told him where the Cayenne was, that the keys to Siao Lin's car were in the ashtray and where it was. I added I'd be on my own for a while. He went quiet, knew straight away what I meant. I took a cab to the airport, no one followed us. We had a small car there which I took and drove to Una's place, parking a block away. Probably shouldn't have, but it seemed the right thing to do at the time. After all, I did want to see Una again, I liked her, and I reckon she liked me, despite the rough way she showed it.

Una was on the defensive right from the start, which I hadn't expected, guess she could tell how I was intrigued by Siao Lin. It was also obvious that Siao Lin right away presumed Una and I were a couple. In the end Una and Siao Lin shared the bed and I slept on that too bloody small couch again. Way worse when you're sober and realise how small it actually is.

23 — Cobalt Trails

'Have a look at this,' said Hugh as he walked into the old man's office. He moved straight across the room and flicked the stapled pages around and down onto the desk in front of the director, turning them in flight with so the appropriate page was the right way round.

'More gold?' asked Harry Browne after a few seconds of perusal. He read further down the page and nodded.

'Hmmm. Interesting,' he mused, looking up at Hugh for the first time. 'Where is it exactly?'

'As you can see, it's in the northern Flinders Ranges,' said the wiry geochemist. 'I checked where the claim was filed, through the Department of Mines records, and it seems to be smack bang on the edge of the Adelaidean metasediments and their contact with basement rocks. Quiet near an old copper mine named Wheal Frost.'

'What does your information supposedly imply then?' asked Harry.

'Well, that's the question isn't it.' Hugh sounded cautious, which as Harry knew was unusual for such an impulsive character.

Hugh described a report by H.Y.L. Brown, around the turn of the century. He spoke of gold diggings in the area, which he suggested predated the old copper mines; possibly excavated by a Chinese miner or miners, apparently even before Europeans reached the area.

Harry asked if the cobalt could have come from around that area. Hugh said it was unlikely, and it simply wasn't a suitable environment for gold to be found in either. He mentioned that only one soil sample, of thousands taken, during surveys in the seventies, was found to be high in cobalt. It was fifty kilometres away and despite numerous attempts, could never be reproduced and was put down to a sampling error.

'Where was the cobalt rich sample you mentioned found then?' asked Harry, suddenly sounding a bit more interested.

'I think that is the right question,' agreed Hugh. 'Nowhere near where the gold claim is registered at all, it was somewhere up along the eastern edge of the ranges.'

They went on to discuss the fact that the cobalt had entered the gold around the time the gold was deposited. Hugh speculated that either they came in together or the bedrock around the gold was already rich in cobalt. Though Harry Brown was the director of AMDEL, an analytical company with a supposedly high degree of security, he had a mandate from the government to report on any unusual finds of minerals. Cobalt was one of the highest priorities on his list, and he immediately made a mental note to email details to the Organisation.

Harry's desk phone rang once. He picked it up to talk to the receptionist.

'Send them up to my office right away; we were just talking about that claim.' He looked at Hugh whose eyebrows had raised themselves in query.

'There's a Chinese geologist by the name of Siao Lin Wayne here to see us in relation to the gold and cobalt.' Harry said to Hugh, who would have queried him, had it not been for Harry's hand raised to stop him.

'She's in the company of a guy from the Organisation.' he added. 'Something big going on it seems.'

Harry didn't notice Hugh's sudden look of discomfort at his mention of the organisation.

A tap on the door preceded the receptionist entering, she was followed closely by Siao Lin and Russell. The receptionist introduced them and left.

'What can I do for you,' said Harry, smiling.

'We need to borrow some of your equipment for a few hours,' said Russell.

Siao Lin produced a large lump of solid gold, there was a small area of dark rock attached to the nugget.

'What's the bedrock?' asked Hugh, stepping forward. 'Calc Silicate?'

'Looks a bit like it doesn't it,' admitted Siao Lin. 'More likely to be…'

'Sorry to cut in on you girl,' said Russell. 'Director, can we talk to you alone please. No offence,' he turned to face Hugh who was still somewhat goggle eyed, already holding up a silver magnifying glass, obviously trying his hardest to get a good look at the sample. 'I've got my orders.'

Harry ushered Hugh out of the office and turned back to face his two visitors. He walked back around his desk and sat, asking them to do the same.

'What do you need?' asked Harry, still smiling.

I need to have a couple of slides cut from this sample and then I need to use a microscope to examine them,' said Siao Lin. 'We need to identify the bedrock.'

'We need to keep a lid on this for the time being Harry,' said Russell, holding the man's gaze.

'Not a problem,' he replied. 'Can you cut the slides yourself?'

'I can,' agreed Siao Lin.

'Lab three has all you need and it's not being used at present.' Harry stood and walked to the door. 'Follow me, I'll show you where to go.

Russell and Siao Lin followed him into the corridor.

'Is this a national security issue?' he asked, turning to face Russell.

Russell nodded. 'It is indeed,' he said. 'At least for the time being. I don't need to tell you about the leaks from this establishment in the recent past.'

'We're working on it,' said Harry as he preceded them into the office.

Siao Lin looked around and quickly made her way to a bench, on which were scattered numerous pieces of equipment, including a diamond saw.

'This is exactly what I need,' said Siao Lin, turning to smile at Russell.

'I was wondering how you have so much of the sample material and not appear to know where it comes from?' asked Harry, obviously intrigued.

'A good question,' agreed Russell, putting an arm about the director's shoulder and shepherding him toward the door. 'One I'll make an effort to answer as soon as I possibly can Harry.'

'Oh Harry,' said Russell as he stood by the door. 'Call a meeting and tell your staff that whatever deals you've had with mining companies in the past are cancelled for the time being. We're actively keeping an eye on things for the moment.'

Siao Lin was already prepping the saw and undoing the clamp to hold the sample she was ever so anxious to cut.

24 – Visits

Siao Lin cut six slides and had a good look at them through the back lit microscope. Surprisingly, the rock had begun its life as a lava flow and, judging by the amount of metamorphosis it had undergone, was a good deal older than the nearby Adelaidean rocks. She could only assume the bed was part of the Curnamona group, a small pyroclastic event, of an age with the rocks in the Broken Hill area. The lava flow had occurred around 1,600 million years previously. The gold appeared to have infiltrated the rocks more recently, in the order of 1000 million years ago.

She spoke to Harry as they left and told him she'd left some larger samples for carbon dating and smaller chips, in sample bags, to be run through for cobalt. Russell made sure Harry understood these samples were to be kept secure; only personnel directly engaged in the crushing and analysis were allowed access to them.

Harry took the samples and ensured the room was securely locked. He arranged for security to keep a close watch as well. Siao Lin asked if she could melt the gold free of its contaminants and Harry was only too happy to oblige. Between the three of them, they separated all the gold, 13.9 kilograms, and bagged up all the extraneous material. A lot of gold.

As they took the lift down, Russell asked Siao Lin how much money she needed for the time being. She appeared slightly embarrassed when she admitted she didn't really need any immediately; she told Russell that she had fifty thousand dollars in her ANZ account. Exminoil had paid her out well.

'You're gonna' have a lot more in it soon,' laughed Russell. 'Over half a million. Do you need any cash at all?'

'I still have about two thousand dollars with me,' she confessed.

Russell shook his head as they left AMDEL, Siao Lin was one rich girl. He was sure they weren't tailed as they left, but that was to be expected. Tomorrow would be a different story altogether, word would get out. He ran the small car into Una's tiny, dilapidated garage and closed the door.

Una wasn't home. As soon as they walked into the lounge

room he asked Siao Lin to sit down. She sat and looked at him expectantly.

'How much more work will you need to do on the samples?' he asked.

'Another day,' she replied. 'Less actually, a few hours should be enough.'

'I don't want us to have to go back to AMDEL Siao Lin,' he admitted. 'The first day we got away with, it was unexpected, but if we go back tomorrow, they'll be ready and waiting. I can't take a chance they'll find this place, wouldn't be fair to Una.'

'You're right,' agreed Siao Lin straight away. 'Just get me a microscope and I can do the work here easily enough.'

Rather than try to explain what she needed to Russell, she made a list of exactly what she required. If he could fetch everything the following day, she could quickly do the petrological examinations she would need to further identify the samples. Russell walked out and made a few calls while Siao Lin dug out the geological map she had taken from AMDEL and spent some time looking at it.

'There are only a couple of possibilities,' she said as Russell entered the room a few minutes later.

He turned his head in query.

Siao Lin launched into a description about why Adelaidean metasediments would be unlikely to contain gold and began listing the reasons it was more likely to have come from the older Curnamona metamorphics.

Russell grinned and held his hand up to stop her continuing. He mumbled something about not having a clue what she was talking about.

The following morning was windy and damp, with rain showers sweeping in from the southwest. Russell opened the curtains and looked out after they'd finished breakfast. Siao Lin was in the shower.

'Can I leave her with you today,' he asked Una. 'Take her shopping at West Lakes or Port Adelaide. She could do with some more clothes.'

'Where will you be going then?' she asked, not sounding too keen to nursemaid Siao Lin.

'I've got to get some things sorted for her.' Russell hefted Siao Lin's heavy backpack onto his right shoulder and handed Una a wad of hundreds. 'I have to get her a microscope, need some more cash too. Get some stuff for yourself; receipts will be good if you can get them.'

'All this cloak and dagger stuff is getting to me a bit,' Una admitted, sounding apprehensive. 'Are we in danger?'

'I've been super careful so far,' said Russell. 'If I thought there was the slightest chance of compromise, we wouldn't have come back here. As far as the shopping goes, so long as Siao Lin doesn't use her bank cards she's untraceable. She seems pretty good at being careful herself. I will tell you what's going on, but not for now. Better if you don't know. I'll make it up to you.'

'I'll make sure you do boyo'.' Una was smiling.

Russell dropped the girls off at West Lakes Shopping Centre and drove away into the drizzling rain.

As soon as they walked into the shopping centre, Una suggested a coffee at a little shop in the heart of the complex. Siao Lin had green tea, found it a bit weak, but enjoyed the sweet pastry. They both benefitted from the rest and the realisation that they were on their own time and not being rushed along by Russell. As they chatted easily, Una admitted she couldn't help but wonder what was going on. Siao Lin told her a little; explaining how she was trying to locate where her ancestor had found some gold. She also mentioned that several mining companies were also interested in the location, hence all the secretive stuff. Una laughed it off, saying she wouldn't tell Russell she knew anything.

'He'll be happier if he thinks me ignorant,' they shared a laugh and hit the shops.

Later, after they'd taken a cab to Pt. Adelaide and were enjoying lunch, Siao Lin borrowed Una's phone, and called her new friend in Port Pirie. Mae Ling was going to visit Adelaide, on the weekend, to stay with her family. Siao Lin agreed to meet her, saying they could arrange a place and time on the day, also mentioning she would likely have her bodyguard tagging along.

Russell turned up that evening with the equipment Siao Lin had asked for.

'I had a meeting with your old boss, Pete Millar,' he said, as he placed the heavy flight case containing the microscope on the floor.

'What did he have to say for himself?' asked Siao Lin.

Russell mentioned Peter had been very apologetic and did have a good enough explanation. Apparently, the gold miner Russell had got information from, Neville Horne, had been out drinking and bragging, on nights prior to Russell's visit. The test results had been leaked by AMDEL to several mining companies, meaning there were mining company agents coming out of the woodwork. Maybe some drugs had been slipped into his drink, apparently he was talkative enough. He was manipulated into admitting he knew the gold was stolen from a hotel somewhere in Coffs Harbour. Neville had apparently thought it was a great joke. Once the information was gained by an agent of Exminoil, Peter was contacted. They knew your room had been burgled and figured that was where the gold had come from.

The following day Siao Lin examined the rocks and recorded the details. She was feeling more positive of the rough location of the gold; it almost had to be further north, on the eastern side of the mountains.

Russell told her he was interested in what sort of rock it was, but only if he could understand what she was talking about.

Siao Lin explained it had been a lava flow, probably down the side of a volcano, and possibly one quite close to a sea or an inland lake.

'I can fathom that alright,' said Russell

'No doubt about it,' she said to Russell animatedly. 'It's a highly metamorphosed lava, one sample must have been near the edge of the flow as there are grains of more acidic rocks entwined with it.'

'Is that significant?' asked Russell, probably with little idea what she was talking about again.

'Actually, I'm fairly confident I know where it came from,' she said, not quite sounding convinced. 'I will need to take the microscope with me, just in case, but with luck we'll find the bed it came from if not the gold itself without having to do much testing.'

'Taking the microscope is not a problem,' said Russell. 'Anything else you need, just tell me, I'll make sure it's aboard.'

'You seem like a nice guy Russell,' she looked at him.

'You're mistaken Siao Lin. I'm not in any respect a nice guy,' he admitted returning her gaze. 'This is my job, simply a job.'

Siao Lin told him about Mai Ling arriving the following day and how she'd really like to meet her. Russell seemed taken aback a little and mentioned that she needed to tell him about such things as soon as she learned of them. He then suggested they all go and pick her up; they could have a day in the Adelaide hills, which should be safe enough.

She agreed with him and said her friend was arriving on the train from Pt. Pirie, which arrived at 11.30 am at Adelaide Station.

Una met Mai Ling at the station and showed her where Russell and Siao Lin waited in the car. Siao Lin got out and hugged Mai, then dragged her into the back seat, showing her how much better her ankle was. Russell drove them up to Hahndorf, where they had a nice meal and a few drinks. They drove about the hills a bit, stopping here and there for refreshments. In the evening Russell dropped Mai Ling off at her brother's house in North Adelaide.

Siao Lin decided she liked her new friend even more.

For dinner, at Una's, they ordered in some pizzas, Russell walked around the corner and got a few beers.

'We'll leave first thing in the morning,' he announced when he returned with a carton of Cooper's.

'Where's my car by the way?' asked Siao Lin, suddenly realising she'd almost forgotten about it, so much had been happening. She'd told Russell where she'd parked it, in the central market carpark, and given him the keys when he'd asked for them, but he'd just said it would be taken care of.

'Your car is packed up, fuelled and ready to go,' he was smiling.

'What's the joke then,' asked Una. 'I know that look.'

'It's in Gawler, locked up in a garage,' he seemed pleased with himself. 'My boss Dave dropped it off himself. We'll be secure until we arrive at your claim, then everyone interested will know exactly where we are.'

In the morning, Russell drove the small car northward. They swapped vehicles at Gawler and took the Broken Hill road.

They ate an early lunch at Burra, around 11, and Siao Lin enjoyed telling Russell she'd eaten there previously, after losing him.

Their next stop was at Yunta and they filled all the tanks and ate a greasy roadside snack. They hit the dirt section of the trip around 1.45 pm.

25 — Return to the Mountains

Siao Lin was amazed at the distance they covered, all in the one day. At least they had stopped at Burra, which gave her the chance to show Russell where she'd eaten last time she'd been through there. She got a buzz out of rubbing in the fact that she had so easily evaded the country's most sophisticated surveillance system during her earlier sojourn. Mostly Russell just kept on driving, saying little. She would have stopped more often, still, she had to admit, it was a good way to get somewhere quickly.

From Yunta to Arkaroola was a long and dusty stretch, flat and monotonous for her the second time around. At least driving kept me occupied the first time, she thought. Siao Lin did see a lot more of the scenery; several times they passed distant cattle stations which she hadn't noticed previously. Three times Russell stopped and each time she got out, opening and closing a gate. In the late afternoon, once the Flinders Ranges came into view, the country became more interesting.

Siao Lin found herself wondering yet again how her great great grandfather had managed to cross this wasteland. Even in the company of natives, it must have been a sore trial. It was just so dry.

At Arkaroola she again began to appreciate the mountains. Russell appeared to know Doug, whom she'd spoken with on her first visit. Neither she nor Russell seemed to feel any urgency in getting to where they were going, so they booked a couple of rooms in the hotel, and even signed up for a tour the following day.

Their personal flight the following morning was impressive, and Siao Lin was surprised to learn Doug was not only a member of the family who actually owned the village, but a pilot as well. He also had an excellent knowledge of the general geology of the area and an even better one of the history of local mineral discovery. Doug flew them northward, toward the dark mass of the Freeling Heights. Siao Lin drew a deep breath as an eagle flashed by, not at all far from their flight path. They flew across the deep, twisted gash of the Yudnamutana creek and across the surface of the Freelings. She was amazed by their flying over the edge of the plateau itself. One moment the land surface was flashing by, seemingly only metres below the plane. Then suddenly with no warning, they flew out, over a near vertical drop off, and the Cessna was diving down steeply, toward the ground, seven hundred metres below.

They flew over the area she wished to investigate at several varying heights and although she didn't use her geological maps to orient herself, the process certainly gave her a good perspective of the overall area and what to expect during the days to follow.

After they'd returned to Arkaroola, Russell spoke to Doug in private for a while, as Siao Lin sat out on the grass by the pool. Once the sun set, the temperature dropped quickly, and she spent an hour in her room, poring over the detailed geological map, remembering what she'd seen from the air and aligning the two as best she was able.

Over dinner, Russell suggested driving up the eastern side of the ranges but Siao Lin was adamant she would rather explore from a base near the Wheal Frost, where she had camped previously. Russell accepted her decision, but said he wasn't happy at how exposed it left them. They spent a second night at Arkaroola, Russell downing more than a few beers at the bar, whilst Siao Lin was content with juice and water.

On arrival in the Yudnamutana Valley the following morning, they found a low cloud base had rolled in, hiding the mountain tops. Clouds were streaming, just like waterfalls, along the full length of an extended wall of cliffs; tendrils of misty fog dropped and partially dissolved before being rushed along the valley, swirling in the gusty, cold wind.

Russell took a track, further along the small valley, which Siao Lin hadn't yet travelled. As they passed the dark spire of the cockscomb, several yellow footed rock wallabies leaped off the pinnacle of jasper like rock, dropping down at least ten metres before landing with springy bounces. They bounded off, vanishing quickly between a spattering of round leafed, mallee gums.

The humpy, overgrown track they drove along soon ended, its way barred by a dark fault zone, where ferruginised, silicified material cut across the softer actinolitic bedrock, discontinuously dividing it from the older quartzites of the basement. They climbed the outcropping and from its top got a great view down into the valley of the Yudnamutana Creek. The tree lined creek bed was a hundred metres lower, with the looming, dark plateau of the Freeling Heights beyond and above.

'See that big rocky hill in the middle there?' asked Siao Lin, pointing.

'Everything is bloody rocky,' said Russell.

'The Wheal Frost mine is on the back of that ridge and the valley to the left is where we are headed.'

'How do we get down there?' asked Russell. The valley was a long, steep way below them and there was no way they could go on, the way they were looking.

'A track leads off a creek that runs into this valley, a couple of kilometres back,' she said, pointing back the way they'd come.

'Let's go then,' Russell turned and headed for her car. 'You may as well drive; you seem to know the way.'

Half an hour later, as Russell got out to open a gate, a huge wedge-tailed eagle ran along the track away from them and lifted, albeit laboriously, into the air. It struggled to gain height, soon vanishing behind a ridge of broken quartzite.

'That one was almost too big to be a bird,' he said, as he got back in after closing the gate. 'Biggest wedgy I've ever seen by a mile.'

Siao Lin nodded, agreeing. Her hair had stood on end when she'd seen it was a bird, initially thinking it a person standing by the roadside. The harsh beauty of the scenery was once again having an impact on her, and adding further to her appreciation of what Tamo had written about the area.

After descending a steep, rocky trail and following a stony creek-bed a further three kilometres, they set up camp; two tents, close together, well up out of the creekbed. Siao Lin was aware that Russell was watching her a lot of the time. Still, she trusted him, but just wasn't at all sure whether she liked him watching her so intently. She walked up to the pits dug by her ancestor and looked about. Her claim pegs were intact, seemed like no-one had visited the place at all. She heard a scrunch of gravel and turned.

'Reckon we need to do a bit of work here girl,' said Russell, observing her from a few metres away. 'It oughta' look a bit more like a spot we've found a bit of gold recently.'

26 — Threats

Hugh lived quite close to the AMDEL offices in Thebarton. It was also an easy walk to the little pub he visited most weekends. He didn't often drink mid-week, but being excluded from the petrological examination of the samples he had been dying to look at galled. He knew he was one of the best at what he did; no matter how good the young Chinese geologist was, she could never hope to have a tenth of his experience. There seemed no other option but the pub.

As usual, he smoked a fag as he walked there, new laws were a pain, drink and smoke had always gone together, but there was no getting around them. He threw the butt onto the ground as he turned right onto Port Rd, making a cursory effort to stomp it out with his shoe.

In the pub he ordered his usual, a double shot of Jamieson's and a small beer. He sat by the window, absently watching cars whizz by. The voice from behind startled him; he jerked in fright.

'Sorry to disturb you,' said the Chinese man, not looking at all sorry as he sat down opposite Hugh. 'Can I talk to you a moment?'

'Nothing for you,' mumbled Hugh, knowing exactly what the man wanted. Last person he'd expected, but on reflection, he shoulda' known.

'Just a few words Hugh,' said the man.

'I can't tell you anything,' he said realising he didn't even know the Chinese man's name. 'Security is aware of what's been going on. We've been well warned. The bloody Organisation turned up. Leave me alone, please.'

The man dropped a thick envelope on the table. Hugh knew what was in it, knew well he could use it to pay some of his debts.

'I don't want it,' he forced himself to say.

'Not good enough Hugh,' said the man, leaning across the table. There was no-one near enough to hear.

'This is a threat Hugh.' He spoke evenly and softly, despite the severe nature of his words. His gaze was relaxed and unflinching. 'All your former collusions will be revealed to the authorities, they will learn about your gambling. They will learn about other things far less pleasant.'

Hugh knew the man was serious. He pleaded with him; he really didn't know where the girl had got the samples; hadn't even been allowed to examine them. Grabbing for straws, he mentioned an old soil sample which had assayed high in cobalt. The Chinese agent grabbed at it like a terrier the moment Hugh mentioned it.

Where it had been taken, he asked, and when. The man produced and unfolded a copy of a section of geological map. He pointed out to Hugh where the girl had staked her claim. Hugh shook his head. There wouldn't be gold or cobalt in that pod of Adelaidean rocks.

'Never going to happen,' he told the agent. 'Can't be any gold there.'

'Where was the high cobalt reading from? Where?' The man was insistent.

He pushed the map across the table and handed Hugh a pencil. Hugh marked an area a little north of Paralana hot springs with a large circle. He couldn't remember exactly where it had been, probably a lot further north, he wasn't giving the man any real detail. He mentioned that numerous soil samples had been taken in an attempt to duplicate the reading, but no other high cobalt readings were ever found. They had then presumed the original sample must have been contaminated during the crude analysis procedure used onsite in those days.

The Chinese agent tapped the thick envelope. Hugh shook his head, but knew he'd take it.

'Just leave me alone,' pleaded Hugh. He felt so helpless.

The agent stood, looked down at Hugh like a bug he could step on. He held his position for several seconds, as if considering his options. Hugh saw him shake his head ever so faintly, before walking quickly from the pub. Saw him through the window, sporting a scary, knowing smile, as he zipped his coat against the chill of the street. Within a few seconds a car pulled up for him. He walked to the kerb and got in, the car pulled out fluidly, into the busy Port Road traffic.

Hugh sat for a few seconds. He took the envelope and stuffed it in his coat pocket. He'd check it when he got home. He finished his drink. They'd never leave him alone; the whole situation was well beyond him. Only one thing he could do though, probably a mistake, but he remembered the rough guy from the Organisation. He took out his phone and dialled.

'Hi Bill,' he said as quietly as he could. 'This is Hugh Blizzard, from AMDEL. I spoke to you last week. Need your help. You said to get back to you if anything came up. It sure has, reckon you better get here quick. I'm in the Black and White pub down on Port Road.'

Hugh wandered off to the bar and refilled. May as well be drunk when Bill turns up, he thought.

27 — More Gold

When I looked down into the valley Siao Lin was intending to set up camp in, I could see how hopeless it would be to try and maintain any sort of reasonable security; short of bringing in an army. We looked down on it from a dead end track, which would allow an observer a great view. A good sniper could pick someone off from where we stood.

I let Siao Lin drive in, she knew the way. When I saw just how rugged the track was, I was a little more hopeful. Only way they could effectively sneak up was to walk in. A huge wedge-tailed eagle flew off from the roadside near a gate we went through. I'd thought it was a person when I first saw it. Never knew they got that big. Siao Lin just nodded when I talked about the bird, seemed to be lost in a world of her own. Maybe she's under more strain than I realised. Previously, she'd seemed so cool and in control. She really bloody surprised me when she phoned in Adelaide.

We set up a couple of tents, on a gentle slope, well above the creekbed, just above the narrow, raised floodplain. She caught me looking at her a few times, seemed a bit embarrassed at first. Guess it could be a bit disconcerting, having me staring, so I tried not do it so much, or at least not to get caught. Mind you she never actually looked scared at all.

Once we'd had an early lunch, she walked off, up the valley. I followed her of course, managed to surprise her when she stopped and realised I was close behind. I saw the claim pegs and realised that the two faint indentations in the creekbed must have been where her great, great grandfather had dug some pits. I could see how old they were, as a 40 cm thick native pine, long since dead, had grown smack bang in the middle of one.

'Reckon we need to do a bit of work here girl,' I said. 'It oughta' look like a spot we've found a bit of gold. Looks more like a couple of pits dug a hundred years ago. That big dead tree needs to go too.'

She hadn't seen the claim that way, but once I'd mentioned my idea, seemed to think it a good idea. We spent the afternoon enlarging the pits; digging down a metre into the soft grey-green stuff below the creekbed. The tree was easy enough to push over and remove. We even did one trip up to the old copper mine on the high side of the opposite valley and brought back loads of the vein material from there; Siao Lin had taken my little ploy to heart.

I was already amazed at her wiry strength. Not ashamed to admit it was wearing me out walking up hills with her. Guess I needed the exercise and I sure as hell wasn't going to admit to feeling tired.

The following day, Siao Lin suggested I remain in camp while she walked down to the hotsprings and beyond to fetch some more of the gold her great great grandfather had left. I was still feeling a bit overprotective and said I'd go with her. She said she'd done the trip, there and back, in a day before, added it was a long trek, but thought we'd have no real difficulties. We agreed it was best not to leave the camp alone for too long. I was pretty confident that if anyone was going to turn up it would most likely be at the place she'd filed the claim.

We left early and followed the Yudnamutana Creek downstream. The cliffs to both sides were pretty spectacular, although I felt I needed to keep my eyes on the rocky riverbed, save turning an ankle or something similar. Long before we got through the mountains I was regretting my decision to tag along. Siao Lin kept up a steady pace and I figured her lightness helped her a bit, whereas my extra weight had my footsteps sinking a lot further into the sandy gravel, which was the go, on a lot of the flood banks we traversed. She seemed nimbler than me through the thick growths of ti-tree too.

Not long after we passed some dark looking caves, the mountains drew back and we turned left, out of the creekbed, and onto a gentle spinifex clad slope. That stuff was even spikier than I remembered, I soon learned to expend the extra energy to miss the clumps altogether, avoid those needle sharp spikes. A couple of ridges later, we reached the hotsprings. They looked like a few scummy pools to me; well, they were very steamy, scummy pools, but I wasn't impressed. We kept going, until, about fifteen minutes later, Siao Lin suddenly slipped off her pack, took out a small folded shovel, opened it and began digging next to a large granite boulder.

I helped scoop the soil away from her dig and within a few minutes she began to haul out large lumps of gold. She left a few smaller pieces behind, the rest she loaded into her backpack, which she insisted on carrying, laughing and saying she wasn't going to trust me not to run off with her gold. As if I had that much energy, reckon the pack woulda' been the final straw for me.

Once we got back to the hotsprings, she stripped to her underwear, cleared an area of weedy scum and lowered herself into the steaming water. Looked and smelled pretty dire, but I have to admit, I wasn't far behind. It was bloody hot, and it sure did relax my tired muscles, never was sure I would have got back to camp without that break. We ate a couple of sandwiches for a late lunch and rested a further hour. It was a sunny day, but not particularly hot, at least winter was good for something.

Not long after beginning the long walk back up the Yudnamutana creek, I realised just how tough that girl was; in fact I was absolutely amazed. She carried at least twenty kilos of gold on her back and I was struggling to keep up with her even though I carried almost nothing. Time to get back into shape, I thought as we hit an extra soft patch of sand. My head was reeling with mathematical calculations; 20 kilos was about 700 ounces, worth around three quarters of a million. I added the 550,000 for the first lot of gold and the 100,000 she already had in her account. Ended up with a total of 1.4 million, and there could be more gold too.

It was a bit slower going back up the creekbed. I offered several times to take the heavy pack off Siao Lin, but fortunately she never looked like giving it to me. We got back to camp as the last of the yellow sunshine shone on the mountain above the Wheal Frost copper mine. I vaguely remember Siao Lin cooking some eggs before I was out to it.

The following day, trying hard not to show how tired my legs were, we sorted out the campsite. We buried the gold up the ridge a ways, even used a few tiny pieces of gold to salt the fake claim area. We spent some time discussing Siao Lin's actual search for the location of the gold; she thought the area where she'd find the source of the gold, was a half a day's walk north of the hotsprings. We talked and agreed it would be more logical for her to head off on her own whilst I awaited any newcomers at camp. I didn't mention I was in several minds about the plan. I was actually relieved at not having to do the walk again, and more than a bit horrified that I wasn't up for it physically, even though I was damned uncomfortable at the risk factor as she headed off on her own. I knew it was the lazy option but really did feel it was for the best. I was convinced they'd come in the way we had. Can't always be right though can I?

28 – Good Night Dom

Dominick had just spoken to Frank on the phone, giving him the information as to where Siao Lin had pegged her gold claim. He'd emailed maps and plans earlier and during the conversation told Frank to see what he could do to disrupt whoever was up there in the Flinders Ranges, whilst he would arrange for one of his contacts to claim all the ground nearby with a blanket lease. That should keep the bloody Chinese happy, he thought; maybe they'd pay him the sort of money this job was worth.

He phoned his contact at Zihnjihn and gave them all the relevant information. They didn't seem enthusiastic, probably had what he gave them anyway and he knew from past experience that the Chinese never gave much away. Dominick did ask when he could expect further payment. He hadn't received anything from them since the second payment of $10,000. He'd pretty much used that up paying Frank and his cronies. They simply said they'd send someone. The whole conversation lasted less than a minute.

He put the phone down, just as his door banged open and Bill charged into his office.

'Bill,' said Dominic. He almost said *nice to see you*, but realised it would've been pointless.

'I'm well enough, thank you Dom,' said Bill, looming over the desk. Bill may have been thin but he was tall and wiry. 'You used me. Only my boss telling me to go easy is keeping you alive.'

'Where's Rabbit?'

'He's a bit tied up Dom,' Bill didn't laugh. 'Just you and me.'

'What do you want then?' asked Dominick

'I don't want anything Dom,' said Bill, scratching his head. 'We're well onto you and you'll get what you deserve soon enough, just telling you to leave me alone. Happens again and I won't bother to listen when I'm told to go easy on you.'

Once he'd said his piece, Bill simply turned and walked out. Dominic gave him a minute to get clear and walked through to the back of the shop where Rabbit was well tied to an antique chair. He didn't speak, just untied him and went back to his office. Seems this wasn't going to be a good day at all.

Several hours later, Dominic sat back at his desk, beginning to think that maybe things weren't too bad. His IT sources had uncovered the positioning of the Chinese girl's claim, the source of the gold, and maybe Zihnjihn would look after him eventually, once they saw how much he'd given them. He looked up as he heard a tap on his door. The door opened.

'There's a Chinese fella' here to see you Dom,' said Rabbit, poking his head around the door.

'Send him in Rabbit,' he said. That was quick.

The agent was wearing a black T-shirt and loose cloth belted cotton pants. From the look of him, Dominic knew he wouldn't be worried about the cool weather at all. He wasn't a huge man, but Dom had a notion he would be well able to look after himself.

'We want you to call off your men on the job,' said the stocky Chinese man as soon as he entered. No introductions or anything approaching a nicety at all. 'We have the situation in hand and don't require further assistance.'

Dominick laughed to cover his uncertainty. 'I don't understand. Why would you want my men out? Our agreement was for me to supply the men on the ground...'

'We have men in position and have already filed claims on the areas we need. Your attempts to file a blanket lease have failed. You and your organisation serve no further purpose. You have been paid for your services and we simply require you to withdraw your men.'

'I received two small amounts with promise of further payment, I chose your company to deal with because of what they offered. Anyway, what's your name?' As he finished speaking, Dom touched the button to the intercom so Rabbit could hear the conversation. Times like this he would rather have had Big Frank nearby.

'My name is Ming Sen and I am asking you for the final time,' The Chinese agent spoke slowly. 'Withdraw your men immediately. You may be paid further, that is beyond my control, but you must withdraw your men.'

Dominick shook his head, holding the dark eyes of the small Chinese man. He stood and walked out from behind his desk, in an attempt to show he was unafraid. Suddenly the man had a gun in his hand and it was pointed at his stomach.

'Sit down please,' said Ming Sen, motioning with the weapon.

'No need for a gun?' Dominic held both hands waist high, palms down. His smile didn't indicate how icy he suddenly felt inside. This wasn't going at all the way he liked. He moved back behind the desk, sitting and unobtrusively reaching under the desk for the gun he kept there.

As his fingers found it, Rabbit burst in the door, gun waving as he looked for a target. Unfortunately for him, Ming Sen turned smoothly and squeezed off two accurate, silencer muffled shots. They thudded into Rabbit's chest, he was dead as he crumpled to the floor.

Ming Sen held the gun on Rabbit as he collapsed, watched him for an elongated second. Satisfied Rabbit was dead, he turned back to Dominic, who was just pulling his own gun free of the desk. Ming Sen was way faster. He shot Dominic twice, watched him fall, and left the room, closing the door behind him.

As Ming Sen casually walked from the front of the shop, a car pulled up and he climbed in the back seat. A man stepped out of the other side rear door and walked into the shop. The car did a cautious U-turn and drove away to the west.

At the edge of town, where banana plantations crept in close to the houses in the surrounding foothills, the car dropped the black clad agent and the front seat passenger off at the entrance to one of the plantations. They conversed in Mandarin as they walked to a waiting helicopter, which had started its engine when the car arrived. The chopper lifted as soon as they boarded. It rose barely high enough to miss the banana trees, which bent and flapped about with the down force of the rotors, before climbing steeply to the west, to clear the mountains of the great divide.

29 — Eureka

Siao Lin woke at first light and leapt straight out of her sleeping bag. The air was crispy cold but the gusty wind of the previous day had died away. She poked at the fire, revealing still glowing embers beneath the grey ash, and threw some kindling onto them. Smoke immediately began to curl upward, and by the time she had cut some thick slices of bread the flames were licking and crackling. She toasted four pieces and put a good supply of water in the kettle.

The smell of toast roused Russell. She'd known it would.

'Bloody early,' he mumbled standing in close to the fire and rotating.

'I've got a long walk,' she smiled at him, he looked half asleep. 'All right for some.'

Siao Lin knew well how far it was to the hotsprings and wanted to get an early start, finish her day's walk early and rest up for the walk north on the following day. She ate breakfast quickly as Russell drank his coffee, huddled in close to the fire.

Once she'd packed her backpack, she wandered to the back of the camp, to the north, where a three metre high ridge of siliceous, iron-rich jasper ran for about thirty metres. She climbed to the top of it and began her morning stretching exercises. She was quite enough, but within a few minutes she executed a 180 degree pivot, whilst balanced on the toes of one foot and noticed Russell below, watching intently. Her ankle was still a little sore when it had to take her whole bodyweight, so she finished early and climbed down the steep rock face.

'Looks a bit like Tai-Chi,' said Russell as she neared him.

'Tai-Chi was derived from what I was taught, it is similar, basically a simplified version for the average person.'

Russell nodded and followed as she passed him. She took a handful of dried nuts and sultanas and put them in her pocket. A minute later she was on her way, in search of gold. Russell watched from his camp chair. She noticed the weight she carried and took a few deep breaths. The water-skin was heavy, and the rifle, which Russell insisted she take, was awkward. She swapped them about every few hundred metres, the weight was manageable. Most of the water would be gone by the time she returned in a couple of days anyway.

Russell had asked her to be careful and given her a satellite phone too. She promised to call him in the evening, or earlier if anything untoward happened. Siao Lin was happy to get off on her own and took pleasure in a new found sense of freedom as she walked easily down the riverbed.

Not that she was in any rush. In fact she took her time, investigating everything of interest she could find. She revelled in the heights which soared above her as she followed the meandering creekbed through the heart of the mountains. Despite the weight she bore, it was a less demanding journey than she'd expected; probably because she was taking it easy and resting whenever she felt like it.

She set up her bedroll at the hot-springs the first night, eating some dried fruit and a tin of beans which she immersed in the hot water for ten minutes. Where the water issued from its subterranean labyrinth, it was boiling, so she gathered it must be safe to drink once cooled.

After dark, she used the satellite phone to call Russell and was relieved to hear no visitors had been near camp. On a whim she then called Mai Ling and had a good chat. Mai Ling was glad she called and had some interesting news for her. According to the Chinese nurse's father, word was out that a Chinese man named Ming Sen, well known as an expert in Chinese martial arts, and suspected of underworld contacts, was seeking and willing to pay well for any information about Siao Lin Wayne's present whereabouts. Siao Lin was not surprised, as Russell had already mentioned something similar, in saying that Zihnjihn was their main suspect. Zihnjihn's reputation suggested the use of ruthless greed and corruption to monopolise deposits of exotic and rare minerals worldwide. She was a little worried that word reached her through such a public source as Mai Ling, and hoped she could locate the source of the gold and get out of the area before they decided to come looking.

In the morning Siao Lin walked northward, following the edge of the ranges. She soon passed the place where Tamo had hidden the gold, and a few kilometres further on, came across an area where water was seeping out of the ground. She filled her water skin with the somewhat brackish liquid, knowing the spring was there because of the major fault line which ran along the eastern edge of the mountains. She resolved to check in more detail, next time she dug out the geological map.

That evening she camped by the side of a large, dry creekbed which ran out from the Freeling plateau. The night was cold, but her sleeping bag was up to the task and after the long day's walk, she slept well.

Early next morning, after a quick breakfast, as the sun rose above the desert plains to the east, she walked upstream, along a small tributary creek and into a wide valley. One of its edges was rimmed by dark cliffs, and she walked across to investigate. She saw weathered, humpy shapes, and wondered if they could have been pillow lava, before they had been substantially altered by heat and pressure. After chipping a few samples with her pick, she realised that the basic, metamorphosed lava bed was pretty much identical to the samples she had examined recently, through the microscope. Tamo must have found his gold somewhere nearby.

She was about to start more detailed investigations, when several euro's hopped across the valley. She looked back behind as they fled, obviously startled by something further down the creekbed; the same one she had followed to enter the valley. Immediately suspicious of someone following her, she chipped off a quick sample and began walking, not wanting to linger too long and alert them she had located what she had been seeking. As Siao Lin walked across the valley, she passed sunken patches where pits had been re-filled. It seemed Tamo had been here indeed.

In an effort to disguise the fact she'd already found what she sought, she climbed a ridge out of the valley and continued walking further north along the edge of the ranges for an hour. She periodically broke rocks and examined them. Around midday she turned and walked south, back to the hot-springs. Twice she turned her head and noticed glints of light, once in some river gum saplings and a second time on a scrubby hill, overlooking her position. She was almost sure that somehow, someone had found her. She turned off the course she took on the northward leg, and checked out some juvenile mallee gums. On reaching them she saw fresh scuff marks and recent boot prints. Not hers for certain; someone else had been there quite recently. She continued to poke about in different areas for the rest of the day as she walked back south.

She remained alert, but rather than try and lose her follower, she decided to run him about, being in no hurry and figuring that at least then she knew where he was whilst he was following her. She reached the hot springs just before nightfall and set up her swag. She delayed calling Russell, not wanting whoever was following her to be alerted to Russell's presence.

She stripped to her underwear and walked into the hot waters, instantly feeling their soothing heat on tired leg muscles. Ten minutes later, still relaxing in the hot waters, she was startled by a voice. About to reach for the rifle she'd placed on the rock above her, she saw a young aboriginal man in the flickering firelight. At first she thought he was the youth from her visions, but quickly recognised him as the man she had given money to in the park, in Adelaide. He looked quite different with a spear, boomerang and small shield, and wearing a thick cloak of animal skins.

'You bein' stalked missy,' he grinned, teeth bright in the firelight.

'I know,' she whispered, placing a finger to her lips to quieten him.

'He can't hear you. He's way down the creek,' said the aborigine. 'He's very tired, snoring pretty loud. Thinks you be sleepin' too I reckon.'

Siao Lin felt herself relax. She stood from the waters and took the towel to wrap around her. The night air was steamy, but cold after the heat of the water.

'What's your name?' she asked.

'Geoffrey,' he said quietly. 'What's yours?'

Siao Lin wrapped the towel tighter against the night. 'I'm Siao Lin,' she said nodding. 'I remember you from Adelaide.'

'You shoulda' come see me at Nepabunna,' the young black man grinned, his teeth white in the reflected firelight and 'I got tired of waitin'. Walkabout up this way.'

'Thank you Geoffrey,' she said. 'Who is that following me? What does he look like?'

'Bit like you. He's a Chinese man, like you.' Geoffrey nodded, and vanished into the night.

He's a different person up here in the bush, she thought as she called Russell and told him she was being followed. She didn't mention Geoffrey.

Russell wanted to come down in the night but she told him she'd be alright and would head back up to their camp by first light, hopefully leading the Chinese man who was following her to him. She finished by adding that she would call him half an hour before she arrived, in the morning.

Russell agreed, and said he would set up an ambush of sorts, along the way she would pass, but Siao Lin could tell he didn't really believe that she was being followed at all.

30 – Bill

'**Yeh, Dominic bought** it yesterday,' said Dave tapping the fingers of his left hand as he held the phone receiver to his right ear, listening.

'Bill was there two hours before he was killed alright,' he said a few seconds later. 'Who else coulda' done it. I'm gonna' have to suspend him this time.'

His fingers tapped even faster as he listened again.

'Russell, your bloody gut feeling is no good to me on this one.' Dave raised his voice. 'I need a real reason to leave him on the case, I know we have no actual proof but it looks real bad. Sure Dominic deserved it, but we can't go 'round knocking off people just because they deserve it.'

Dave shook his head as he listened to Russell's reply. He told Russell to keep him up to speed and hung up the phone. He heard a noise in the back office and realised some-one else was there. He got up and walked around to investigate. Bill was sitting with his feet up on his desk.

'You got back from Coffs quick enough,' said Dave, trying his best not to look surprised.

'Wasn't me Dave,' Bill said, making no effort to get up or move his feet off the desk. 'First I heard of it was just then, when you told Russ.'

Dave told Bill, in no uncertain terms, that he was under suspicion for the murder of Dominick and might well be suspended, pending the results of an investigation.

Bill slipped into his shirty mood. He told Dave he was sorry for the previous leak he inadvertently caused, but still felt it his duty to help with the situation as best he could. He again denied having anything to do with Dominic's death. Dave was not convinced and detailed the fact that all CCTV tapes from Dominic's shop after Bill tied up Rabbit were carefully erased.

Bill was taken aback by the information. He may have been thinking fast but he looked like a stunned mullet; he held Dave's eyes, but was obviously in some confusion.

'The tapes were erased?'

'Like I said before Bill,' continued Dave. 'The tapes at

Dominic's all end when you walk into the place and tie up Rabbit.'

'I tied Rabbit up alright,' replied Bill, back in gear again. 'But I didn't go near the CCTVs at all. Whoever killed Dominic must've erased them. What was the time of death? Betcha' I was in the Coffs Hotel, well on my way to getting drunk.'

'You pulled the observers away from Dominic's.'

'Yeh, I did, no point them being there when I was threatening him was there.'

'I'm gonna have to suspend you Bill,' Dave held out his hand toward Bill.

'Think about it Dave,' Bill replied, taking his feet from the desk and sitting up. 'If I were going to pop him don't you think I woulda' covered myself. I warned him off is all.'

He asked Dave to consider who did it if he didn't. He raised the all too close to the mark scenario of Zihnjihn on the trail of Russell and Siao Lin. He asked who else would have the knowhow and personnel to do what was done at Coffs.

Bill paused and rubbed the stubble on his jaw, he could see Dave wasn't convinced. He asked him if he'd checked the mining leases around the Yudnamutana area. He stood and walked up to Dave, standing half a metre from him, eye to eye.

'You let Russ go rogue on this one,' he said, explaining he had no real grudge against Russell. He was simply irritated by the way Russell acted so casually most of the time.

'You need to leave me on the job,' Bill said finally. 'I might well be the only one who can help them.'

Dave nodded, Bill's reasoning was kinda' sound, he walked to his desk and began to call up data. A minute later, as Bill waited patiently, back in his seat with his long legs on the desk again, Dave cursed loudly.

'Zihnjihn,' he said. 'They just filed a blanket lease over the whole area between Yudnamutana Valley and Wheal Frost. It's been done through Tazman Gold, but they're owned by Zihnjihn.'

Bill grinned and sat down behind his desk. He took a hand gun from his drawer and slipped it into the holster beneath his jacket.

'Hold on,' called Dave from his office. 'I'll give you the details of where Russell and the girl should be.'

As he walked through to Dave's office, Bill said he knew where they were and asked for the keys to the Cayenne and some guns. Dave threw him the keys and told him there were a couple of rifles in the boot.

Bill caught the keys, nodded and walked out, whistling.

Dave shook his head and returned to his desk where he started punching keys on his computer keyboard. He hoped he'd made the right decision, thought he had. All he could do was wait and see.

31 — Wheal Frost

I spoke to Siao Lin via satellite phone the night after she headed off to seek her elusive gold and cobalt mine. She said she was at the hotsprings and quite comfortable. On her second evening out, she was further north, hopefully close to where her great great grandfather's gold had come from. Siao Lin seemed happy enough, didn't talk much, said she was tired. I wasn't. I'd wandered about a bit, but it'd been a lazy couple of days. I guessed some people would have loved the scenery, and the quiet, but to be honest it bored me shitless. I found myself hoping Siao Lin would locate the place the gold had come from and we could get back to civilisation; if I could finish the job with her, maybe I could get into something a bit more lively and challenging.

When she called, on the third evening, Siao Lin sounded anxious. With her whispering, it was hard to hear, but I gathered she thought someone was following her. I told her I thought it unlikely, but she was adamant, reckoned there was no doubt; she'd seen definite evidence. She also added that the source of the gold had been located, or at least she had found the general area. She planned to walk back toward Wheal Frost, and me, early in the morning.

An hour or so after my late breakfast, Siao Lin phoned again. She was about twenty minutes from camp and was dead sure she was still being followed. Deciding to take her seriously, I told her to walk back to camp and get in amongst the boulders behind the tents with her rifle. I would find a good hiding spot down the creek a little way and watch for anyone following.

I grabbed a rifle to augment my handgun and walked about 400 metres down the creek. I found some large boulders and stashed myself behind them, in a shady spot where I could keep a good watch on the downstream side of the creekbed.

Ten minutes later, Siao Lin came into view, walking quickly. She didn't see me, but spotted my tracks when she reached them. As she drew level with me, she looked about, but kept walking. I stayed hidden and kept my focus downstream as she trudged off toward camp.

Five minutes later, I picked out a figure moving upstream. He was wearing camouflage gear and hunched forward as he walked, watching the trail he was following, but constantly looking up and about. As he got closer, I lost my view of him, but decided to stay hidden. I didn't need to see him, I could hear his footsteps, and besides, I had positioned myself so he'd be in full view once he was level with me. I was crouched down, and small native chicory bushes allowed me to watch through their foliage without being seen.

Thirty seconds later I saw the man clearly, just in time to have him spot my tracks, something I'd not even thought about; been a while since I'd been in the bush. Gotta' hand it to him, he not only spotted my tracks as he reached them, but seemed to know exactly where I was concealed. He looked right in my direction. Couldn't have seen me, but within seconds, he was walking quickly upstream. I thought of standing and calling to him to surrender, but as if hearing my thoughts he turned and swung his rifle toward the rocks I was in. He continued to walk backward, swinging his weapon to and fro.

A minute later, as he climbed across a rock bar which crossed the creek, near 200 metres upstream, I lost sight of him. Beyond, I knew the river bent to the right and there was a bordering of thick ti-tree scrub along its banks.

I slipped out from behind the boulders and followed, walking quickly, hoping he hadn't stopped to ambush me. Once I got to the place I'd lost sight of him, I saw the distance between his footprints lengthen; he'd turned to face forward again and started to run. As I passed where our campsite was fully visible, I saw his trail continue on, up the Yudnamutana Creek. I stayed on his trail, not liking the thought I had about walking into a trap at all. I was beginning to appreciate how hopeless it was up in these mountains, for one man to try and maintain a secure environment. Ten minutes later, as I reached the point where his tracks ran up out of the creekbed, I heard a helicopter. Never sighted it, they must've stayed behind the ridge ahead of me, but I'd seen the man was Chinese, he was obviously well trained, almost definitely working for Zihnjihn. I had a feeling he'd be back though; we'd meet again.

'I saw him run up the creek.' Siao Lin was waiting at camp. 'What do you want to do next?'

'Reckon you've found the place the gold came from?' I asked, half thinking out loud.

She nodded. 'Same rock, almost definitely. I didn't spend long there as I noticed some kangaroos were scared by something or someone.'

'You did the right thing,' I tried to calm her.

'What should we do now?' she asked, not quite as frantic, but obviously still worried.

'That fella' will be back soon enough.' I said. 'No reason for us to be here much longer is there?'

Siao Lin nodded agreement. 'I want to dig out the small microscope and have a bit of a look at the samples I got, just to be on the safe side. I can't cut slides but I reckon I can see enough to be sure. Be finished by tonight.'

'We can pack up tomorrow then. Is the water from the well in the creekbed alright?' I asked. The tank in the Landcruiser had run out while Siao Lin had been off walking.

'I drank some on my first trip here and had no trouble,' she replied quickly. 'It wasn't salty at all.'

'I'll fill up our drums then,' I said, relieved as we were down to the last cupful. I wandered off to get a bucket and some thin rope and draw up water from the deep well on the lower floodplain, at the junction of the two rivers

That night we ate a hearty stew, the well-water proved to be sweet and potable. I didn't worry about keeping lookout, figured the helicopter had flown off south and wouldn't be back for a while.

32 — A Testing Time

The following morning, Siao Lin and Russell woke feeling stomach pain and nausea. They ate a small breakfast and within half an hour they both had to rush off and throw up. The accompanying stomach cramps quickly became more severe and their half-hearted attempts at packing up camp ceased altogether. By afternoon, diarrhoea began too. Trial and error soon showed them that whenever they ate or drank, even water, they would vomit within minutes.

They carried a basic first aid kit, but it held nothing which would have any effect on whatever they had, nor had they much inclination to do anything at all. They spent the latter half of the day between sleeping and moaning at the more severe stomach cramps.

During the long night following, they were both forced to get up numerous times. Once in the early hours of the morning, Russell, wearing thongs, was stung on his bare foot by a large scorpion. He had trodden on its head and it had flicked its stinging tail up, lodging into the softer skin between heel and ankle. Siao Lin helped him extract the stinger with half of the creature still attached.

Their fevers raged for a further two days and though they were aware of their situations, they were too weak to attempt to leave the area. Walking was difficult and seemed to encourage the stomach cramps to worsen. Russell's leg swelled up as far as his knee for a day and then got very, very itchy.

Early on the third day of their sickness, Siao Lin was squatting in the creekbed, trying to breathe deeply and relax despite the pain. She knew that they were both dangerously dehydrated; neither of them had been able to even keep water down. In the morning sunlight, beyond a row of spiky spinifex bushes, the mauve and black petals of poppies formed a bright backdrop.

Opium? It was an ancient remedy for amoebic dysentery, she thought. We could have got it from drinking the well water. She entered Russell's tent and sat beside him. He stirred and either smiled thinly or grimaced. She told him of the opium and of its stomach sterilising properties.

'Do you know how to get opium from the poppies?' he asked.

Siao Lin nodded. 'I think so, I mean, I've read about how it's done. We'll need something very sharp.'

'There's a scalpel in the first aid kit,' said Russell, tensing as he hunched down and gripped his abdomen.

In the afternoon, despite feeling drained of energy, Siao Lin wandered haphazardly down the banks of the creekbed, thinly slicing poppy bulbs as she passed. Russell followed her course an hour later, in the evening, scraping the drying fluid from the bulbs, a mixture of pasewa and opium. Rather than wait for the opium to separate from the more poisonous material, they simply ate the dried juices, finding the taste very bitter and unpleasant. They were afraid to drink any water with it, or eat anything else, lest they vomit and waste the opium.

Not long after they'd eaten the bitter drug, less than an hour, they felt tired and dreamy. Stomach cramps continued, but felt increasingly distant. Siao Lin sat with Russell, inside his tent and they were both well under the influence of the opium; dreaming in snatches whilst they were still awake. They both realised how thirsty they were, and deemed it time to drink. Initial cautious sips of well-boiled well water turned to gulped mouthfuls once they realised they weren't going to be sick. Neither of them felt like eating at that stage, so they lay and dreamed, partially asleep but at times awake and fully conscious. Around midnight, as the bright full moon reached its zenith, they both fell into sleep.

The visions of the night were intense for Siao Lin. After a seeming age of chaotic dream, she was awoken in her sleep by a giant, so huge his feet straddled the mountains. When she first became aware of him, he was tearing off huge slabs of stone, whole mountain tops, and throwing them about, roaring with laughter. Suddenly, awareness of being watched turned his features. The giant looked down at her. He saw them both in the tiny tent. Siao Lin could sense limitless power. He laughed and massive boulders rumbled down mountain sides, shaken loose by the thunderous rumbling. She felt the cut of extreme fear, as it sliced away all her layers of protection. This was no benign being; awareness of him awoke his awareness in return, and imparted knowledge of the depth of his power.

Siao Lin squinted to see him so far above. His eyes shone with the effortless comprehension of her innermost feelings, causing him to laugh again. The mountains continued to shake and she knew that even the great snake Arkaroo had turned to hide, deep in his Gammon home. The eyes of the giant gleamed with intelligence and knowing; Siao Lin, in her turn, felt recognition. She was aware of the aboriginal youth she'd dreamed several times previously; he was a tiny part of the giant. Despite his power and alien nature, Siao Lin felt unexpected openness and honesty; a deep desire to change her, along with an unlimited willingness to be changed. She found sudden respect for the giant tempering the terror, or at least making it bearable. As she relaxed, and her initial fears took flight, she moved further into him, realising he was a sort of composite. A multitude of characters; the chaos of thousands blended within, never quite at war, always moving, ever changing. There were so many encompassed, it was beyond her understanding. She smiled as she ceased trying to define the Giant and became part of his consciousness.

Siao Lin saw through his eyes, felt the being's presence and saw his vivid memories; she felt the faintest trace of her ancestor. Tamo was there too. In a moment she saw all of her ancestor's long, long life. Then she was swept aside, feeling tiny fletches of so many individuals; so many of the people; aborigines who had known this consciousness, and in turn become part of it. Those who had cared for the land now lived in the dream she had been allowed to share. He was the ultimate protector of the land, unknown by the vast majority of men and women, yet with such power; nevertheless so subtle; beyond reckoning. As Siao Lin drifted into dreams and deep sleep, she knew at last, exactly what the young aboriginal man was referring to when he said she must continue seeking.

In the morning, at first light, they awoke together, lying in each other's arms. They felt drained and weak, but without cramps. They quenched extreme thirst, kissed and touched each other, at first in relief, and then with need. Their feelings were intense. They made love in a slow, passionate frenzy. There was no initiator, unless there were two simultaneously; seemingly both were intensely attracted to the passion of the moment. Later they fell asleep. Side by side, wrapped loosely, they drifted into a deep and dreamless sleep. An hour later they awoke again, both revelling in not feeling sick. They were ravenously hungry.

Without speaking, they separated, each heading off to relieve themselves, to wash and dress. The last of the bread was toasted, eaten with old butter and vegemite, along with green tea. Russell complained about the lack of coffee, but they were both happy to be able to eat something and keep it down. Memories of the dreams of the previous night seeped through between Russell's memories of them making love.

'I dreamed of one hell of a giant,' he remarked as he remembered.

'Did you see the giant too?' asked Siao Lin, surprised, she'd thought she'd had that vision alone.

'Pretty scary eh?' said Russell, not seeming surprised they'd shared the same vision. He couldn't easily forget looking up at those malevolent eyes, a kilometre or two above. An involuntary shiver shuddered through him as he looked up at the deep blue sky, half expecting to see the giant again.

'I think there was more to that dream than I remember,' he admitted, laughing off a faint miasma of fear, and shifting his thoughts successfully to Siao Lin, sitting in the morning sunlight beside him.

Siao Lin laughed too. She wasn't covering up any fear, and there were no regrets either.

They sat back in the camp chairs, feeling drained and weak, but pleasantly full of toast. Russell felt he had to bring up what had happened between them, half felt he'd taken advantage of Siao Lin. She laughed again, louder than previously. She looked at him and asked seriously if he thought he could have done what he did if she didn't want it too. Russell was happy to admit she was right. He knew he kept forgetting what she was capable of. Russell went quiet then, half wondering if Siao Lin's attitude suggested what had happened had no lasting significance.

A few minutes later, he reminded her they had been set to head south before becoming sick. Siao Lin nodded but seemed lost in thought. Russell suggested they could still pack up and get back to Adelaide by late that night.

He finished speaking and looked up to see big Frank, standing twenty metres away, holding a rifle, one aimed at him. That driller was with him, Roy, one of those who'd attacked Siao Lin on the drilling platform, and another dark haired guy, an unknown man who looked to be of Italian descent. All three were armed and already had the drop on them, they hadn't heard a vehicle; nor noticed the sound of any footfalls until it was well too late.

Frank was on the narrow track they'd worn in since arriving there. The dark fella' stepped a few paces to Frank's right and the big driller remained close to Frank's left side, a pace or so behind him.

'Dominick is dead Frank,' said Russell, standing and looking around.

'That's funny,' Frank wore a faint grin as he spoke. 'We got a message from Dominic a few days ago, in person. He told us exactly where you were.'

'I bet a man with a Chinese accent relayed the message?' Russell asked, grasping at straws. Not much else to do, his gun was in the tent, he wouldn't risk Siao Lin to grab for it.

'Can I shoot her now Frank?' asked the big driller holding the shotgun.

'We need what's in her head,' said Frank turning his head to face the man. 'Just keep 'em covered for now.'

'Dominick gave us directions,' Frank was smiling in an odd way. 'But a Chinese accented man did try to talk us out of coming here this morning. I couldn't get through to Dom to check on him at all. How did you know about the Chinese accent?'

'Zihnjihn was financing Dominick,' said Russell, stretching as if he was a whole lot more relaxed than he actually was. 'Must've had a disagreement with him. Heard they popped him a few days ago. Chinese man was wandering about here recently, thought that was how you knew the layout.'

'We used a map,' said Frank, lowering his gun. The other two didn't follow suit. 'Drove to where we figured you couldn't hear us. Long bloody walk in too. Anyway, say I half believe you Russ? What do you expect me to do?'

'You know who I work for Frank,' Russell spoke as seriously as he could manage, knowing Frank was reasonable; he was too smart not to see his point and he just might give it up. 'You think they're gonna' let you get...'

Suddenly the driller lashed out with the butt of his shotgun, striking Frank on the side of the head. Frank's gun skittered across rough gravel, the driller was recovering from the strike he'd made, needing a few more seconds to get the gun back around and aimed. Russell tensed to run and dive forward for Frank's gun, but looked up, to the third man. He had purposefully raised his weapon, keeping it centred. The driller too quickly had him covered again. Frank was tough enough alright, he struggled to stand but the driller kicked him in the back, sending him sprawling closer to where Russell stood. Siao Lin remained seated on the camp chair, he caught her eye and saw her nod ever so faintly.

Siao Lin stood up, lifted the water jug and stepped toward Frank who was barely two metres from them.

'Easy girl,' said the driller. 'Shooting you before you tell us where the gold is 'aint gonna' upset me too much. I 'aint drunk this time.'

She looked at the driller as she splashed water on Frank's head-wound.

Russell took a step toward the two men; he was right beside Frank's gun, and as he'd hoped, both guns were on him. Frank eased out of Siao Lin's helping hands to stand beside him.

Seeing Russell stop, the driller took aim at Siao Lin again. I knew he might well shoot her, and was on the point of jumping in front of her and pushing her back. The dark man had his gun lowered, pointing at Russell's feet, he didn't seem quite so keen on what was happening by that stage, Frank must've hired him, thought Russell. Reckon he'd up and shoot quick enough if need be though; his eyes were glued on Russell and he looked tense.

A shot rang out. The driller dropped, shot through the heart, dead before he hit the ground. A second shot rang out, following the first before its echoes had ceased bouncing around the mountains. Good marksman, thought Russell. Who the hell was it? The other man dropped his gun and buckled down, shot in the leg. The echoes of the gunshots reverberated around the mountain walled valley for several more seconds before being drowned out by pleas and moans from the dark man, who collapsed further, writhing, clutching his thigh.

Bill wandered up from where he had been lying behind a jumble of jasper boulders on the far side of the main creekbed.

'Suppose you're gonna' complain I shot him with no warning now are you,' he said, looking at Russell still standing like a shag on a log.

Russell thought about bending to pick up Frank's fallen gun, but decided he was too tired and weak, and simply stepped back to his chair and sat down. 'I don't give a shit how you did it Bill,' he said. 'Makes us even in one respect at least.'

Bill laughed; rolled the driller's body over with his foot to be sure he was dead. The other man was breathing heavily, but was occupied in keeping too much blood from leaking out. Siao Lin hefted the water bottle and walked to her Landcruiser, taking out the first aid kit. She walked over to the man and began to wash his leg wound before bandaging it.

'Good to be back in action eh Russell,' said Bill. 'Lucky you changed sides Frank.'

Frank nodded. 'I never had a choice did I? Is Dom really dead?'

'Yeh,' Bill nodded. 'It wasn't us popped him, that's all I know.'

'He had a few enemies alright,' said Big Frank, sitting down in the chair Siao Lin had vacated.

33 — More Arrivals

It was the first time I'd met Bill, Russell had mentioned him a few times and I had gathered he was impulsive. His eyes belied his otherwise jerky demeanour with a depth I hadn't expected. He was a bit like a scarecrow on speed, tall, big boned and rake thin. Straight away he demanded food, reckoned he was 'bloody starving'. After eating, he walked out and brought the Cayenne in to the camp. Frank walked out too and drove back in the Land rover they'd arrived in. There was a body bag in the back of the Cayenne and they put the driller's body into it and loaded it in to the rear of Frank's Landrover. Frank drove off, with George, the wounded Italian man, as a moaning passenger.

Ten minutes later, with a wave of his long-fingered hand, and a roar from the tuned exhausts of the Porsche Cayenne, Bill headed off, back to Adelaide. We'd loaded the gold I'd recovered into his car and he claimed he was gonna' tax it, but I knew he wouldn't. Russell reckoned no charges would be filed, the usual with the Organisation. It didn't officially exist at all.

Guess it was me talked Russell into staying a couple more days. Now that the pressure seemed off, I wanted to get some better rock samples from the valley where the gold had come from. In the afternoon, leaving Russell behind, I walked down to the hot-springs and spent the night there. I felt more than a little tired and decided to take it easy and not push on further north that day; after all, we'd just gotten through several days of debilitating sickness.

The following day I walked the ten kilometres north and had a good look around, finding where my ancestor had actually dug the gold out, despite his covering it over well. I took numerous samples, right across the broad bed of dark rock, as I wanted to be able to determine whether the cobalt was present across the entire valley. If so, there would be the possibility of mining in the future.

With the walking north, I felt a lot better, and decided to return to the hot-springs that day. As I walked past the place Tamo had hidden the gold, I saw the big lizard again, bounding into the shelter of a forest of granite boulders. I called Russell after I'd rolled out my bedroll beside the hotsprings. All was well in camp, he felt a lot better now his strength was returning.

The following morning I walked back up the creekbed to the campsite. Again, I felt a bit weary, but not as drained as expected; almost felt I could do the trip again the same day. Almost. I gave Russell a brief hug and walked down to the well where I washed with a couple of buckets of water. I was thinking of how nice it'd be to have a hot shower as I walked up the dusty footpad to camp.

Russell, sitting close to the fire, watched me enter the tent. I dressed in the last of my clean clothes and heard a scrunch of gravel as I exited the tent. Not again, I thought, as I looked up to see a stocky Chinese man walking into camp. The newcomer appeared unarmed. Russell was already standing and walking forward; I saw him take his handgun from its holster. Initially he didn't point it at the newcomer, but kept it ready.

'My name is Ming Sen,' said the man in slightly accented English. 'You will give me information on the location of the gold and cobalt.' He was smiling easily; not at all fazed by the gun Russell had by then pointed at him.

Russell looked around, obviously aware that there were likely to be several concealed gunmen.

'Yes,' the Chinese man's smile broadened. 'You are quick aren't you?'

Russell stepped straight toward the man, pushing a hand back, behind him, hoping I would see his gesture and back off. I just stood there. Unexpectedly, the man jumped in two steps, straight toward him, and very quickly. Russell's gun was knocked from his hand. Ming Sen's other arm snapped across his throat. Russell tried to raise his own arms, but he'd been far too slow and landed with a breath-taking thump, flat on his back. The Chinese man was standing above him, foot on his throat. Russell knew well enough not to move.

The man stepped back. Russell twisted his head to look at me as I took two quick steps forward, to stand beside him. I had assumed a light defensive posture without thinking.

I saw Ming Sen's eyes widen as he noted my stance. He stepped back and lifted his hand, two bullets thudded into the dirt a metre in front of us. Half a second later, gunshots echoed about the valley yet again.

'You have tried to trick us with your claim.' His smile gone, Ming Sen was glaring. 'I want the real location.'

Russell struggled to his feet, opting for silence. A man with an automatic slung over his shoulder was walking up toward us from the creekbed. I saw Russell looking about the mountain slopes above us. My peripheral vision caught movement away up above the Wheal Frost mine, in the jumbled boulders at the top of a broad scree slope. I turned my head, focused for a second and made out a man in camouflage. There could be several more, for we were overlooked from almost every direction.

'You will take us to the location,' continued Ming Sen, looking at me.

'I will take you,' I agreed, standing straighter, losing my defensive posture.

'It is through the ranges isn't it?' asked Ming Sen, pointing down the Yudnamutana creek to the east.

I nodded. 'Half a day's walk.' I said, turning to Russell and winking the eye Ming Sen couldn't see.

'Secure him,' said the Ming Sen as his companion arrived at his side. 'We will leave now.'

'Siao Lin has just walked back from…' began Russell.

'You are still alive Russell Gibb.' Ming Sen regarded him carefully as he stepped closer. 'Do not speak further. You are out of this game. Co-operate and live.'

Ming Sen turned to face the Wheal Frost and signalled. He then pivoted to the south west and repeated the signal, before turning back to regard me. I could see Russell was considering attacking, but the rifle of the agent was centred on him.

'What do you need to take?' asked Ming Sen.

'Just my pack,' I replied.

Ming Sen left only one man to guard Russell, who was by that time tied up securely, as we set off to walk down through Yudnamutana Gorge. Soon two others joined us. They were both carrying heavy packs and automatic rifles. One of them gave a spare rifle to Ming Sen and he threw its strap over his shoulder.

I led them down Yudnamutana Creek, which took about two hours. I then turned northward, walking on past the hotsprings. I dug up the last of the gold stash left by Tamo, a couple of ounces. I was relieved that none of them, as I had hoped, appeared to have any geological knowledge. On seeing the gold I dragged from the pit I'd dug, they appeared convinced I'd shown them its source.

Ming Sen told me his company would find the cobalt now they had its approximate location, adding with a smirk it was a shame I would have to have an accident; after all, these were harsh mountains indeed. I didn't think he was joking, despite his grin. I would take the first chance I got to escape.

By the time we'd walked back to the hotsprings, the sun had vanished behind the soaring massif of the Freeling Heights; already the air was decidedly chilly. A few minutes after we arrived, Ming Sen swore. I turned at his exclamation, saw him bringing up his rifle and just managed to see two aborigines, holding spears, duck behind boulders, over the top of the ridge. They were about 400 metres distant, on raised ridge of dark jasper to the northwest.

'Get them, get them!' he yelled at his men, dropping his own gun down from his shoulder.

The men turned and moved off, one running smoothly to the left, skirting the jasper boulders of the fault zone, whilst the other angled off right, leaping spinifex clumps, near to where a track ran along a dilapidated fence-line.

I suddenly realised that, for the first time, Ming Sen was not watching me, and he was well within reach. I stepped smoothly in toward him and kicked out with my left foot. The gun flew back behind him as I recovered my footing. He faced me, slipping into an aggressive attack posture.

I took a further step back, flowing into a defensive stance. I knew he had plenty of time to recover his weapon before I could strike him again, should he choose to do so. He confused me by stepping to the left, speaking in mandarin.

'I do not need the gun.' He crouched further, more defensively, looking closely at me and the way I stood.

'Where did you train?' he asked.

'My Uncle taught me,' I replied, also in Mandarin.

Ming Sen ran at me, yelling as he closed.

I evaded his strike and easily enough blocked several kicks and punches. We stepped apart. Ming Sen bowed faintly. I bowed more deeply to him.

'I do not wish to fight you Ming Sen,' I said.

'There is little possibility I will not defeat you,' Ming Sen looked somewhat puzzled, despite the confidence of his words. 'I wish to see if the old ways are as good as the rumour of them suggests.'

He moved in more slowly and again I managed to slip aside from, or block, each attack.

'You are too good Ming Sen,' I said as he stepped back. I was breathing hard and could feel my heart pounding in my chest. The recent sickness had weakened me severely and my strength and co-ordination would soon fade.

'I am too weakened. You are too fast and strong for me to evade much longer. Attack me again at the risk of your life.' I decided as I spoke. I had little choice; defeat could well be my death. If I saw an opening to end the fight I would accept it.

'You are good, but not that good,' he replied, grinning. He did not understand the worlds between us.

Ming Sen ran in two steps. It was a ruse, I stood immobile. He stopped and moved more cautiously, edging to his right. He kicked broadly at my side. I pushed his kick aside and moved back. He thought he sensed fear and weakness in my retreat and leaped forward boldly, aiming a left footed kick at my head. I leaned aside as his foot snapped through the space my head had occupied moments before. Ming Sen flew past. He had overstretched and was blind to me as I turned fluidly and leapt after him. Two steps, then a jump nearly to the height of my own shoulders; I kicked him high on the back of the neck as he began to turn back toward me. My whole body weight jerked his head aside. He crumpled into unconsciousness. I bent and found a pulse; he was not dead but unconscious. I knew his neck was broken.

I picked up his gun and sat on a boulder, I was exhausted. My heart was racing and for a minute or so I was breathing hard. I felt I should walk back up the creek and try to rescue Russell, but knew I hadn't the strength. I would rest a while. A few minutes later Geoffrey and another aborigine walked out of the eucalyptus saplings downstream.

'What happened to the men?' I asked Geoffrey, still gripping Ming Sen's gun tightly.

'No men near here except that one,' they grinned at me as they pointed at Ming Sen, I decided not to ask further on the matter.

'I have to walk back up and rescue Russell,' I said, knowing I could never get through the gorge before nightfall.

'Wally will help him.' Geoffrey was still grinning. 'You stay here for the night, light a fire, nice and warm.'

Wally walked off to the south, angling up across the low ridge and toward the Yudnamutana creekbed. Relieved, I managed to find the energy to nod.

Geoffrey turned and began walking away, and, skirting the steaming waters of the hotsprings, began to walk up the creekbed.

'Where are you going?' I called out.

'If I knew that I probably wouldn't bother,' he replied, as he hooked his long boomerang into the rope which doubled as his trouser belt.

34 — Boomerang

Russell sat through the rest of the day tied to the chair. There was never a chance of working himself loose, he was double tied; that is tied hand and foot, then tied onto the chair. Besides, his guard was watching him continuously, untying him only twice to allow him to relieve himself and eat, before tying him back onto the chair immediately.

The night had seemed to go on forever and though Russell dozed at times, the cold of the early hours cut right through the blanket the Chinese agent had thrown over him.

As the sun rose, it was uncomfortably bright, but more than welcome as it began to soak some of the night's aches away. Russell was partially untied, again, this was both to relieve himself and eat the two pieces of dry bread he was offered. If his Chinese captor spoke English at all, he certainly hadn't bothered to. He tried to use his mobile phone, several times, but wasn't answered. This seemed to be making him nervous.

He re-tied Russell to the chair, then wandered off to where the fire was blazing brightly and stood with his back to the flames, warming himself. He rotated about every minute or so as he chewed on some jerky he'd taken from a jacket pocket. Russell caught a glimpse of movement up beyond the brown rocky outcropping behind camp. His guard was facing the opposite way, and Russell saw the head and shoulders of an aborigine, behind the smooth jasper boulders. The newcomer slipped a finger to his lips and ducked back out of sight.

A few minutes later, Russell saw the aborigine again. This time he stepped out slowly, from behind several spiky leaved bushes, growing on the bank of the Wheal Frost Creek. The Chinese guard was looking at Russell, with the new arrival almost directly behind him. The aborigine took a further step and Russell realised he was swinging back an arm holding a boomerang. He swung the arm forward and loosed the heavy wooden weapon. It flew with remarkable accuracy, arcing almost straight at the Chinese agent. With a tremendous whack it struck him side on in the head, dropping him like a stone. The aborigine stood motionless for a second or two.

On realising his target was down for the count, he walked forward.

He stood over the man a moment and then turned and walked a few metres away to retrieve his boomerang. As he picked it up and slipped it into his belt, Russell realised it was a lot thicker and heavier than any he'd seen previously. He'd not realised a boomerang could be so solid, nor pack such an explosive punch as it struck. The dark-skinned man walked toward Russell and, rather than untie all the knots, extracted a small, sharp knife and cut him free.

'What do you know about the girl?' asked Russell.

'She's alright.' The aborigine's smile was wide between words. 'You should walk downstream to the hotsprings and meet her.'

Russell stretched his arms upward, standing on tip toe and arching his back. Being tied up for a day and a night had left him cramped and sore. He looked downstream and wondered if he was up to walking through all the soft river gravel again. He didn't have a choice, just quickly grabbed a pack and crammed food and water the Chinese man had brought into it. He got his rifle out of the tent too, just in case. When Russell tried to call Siao Lin on the satellite phone, her phone started ringing in her tent. Of course! She hadn't taken it with her; he found her phone and threw it into his pack too.

He set off, walking down the narrow dusty footpath. The aborigine walked beside him, falling into step.

'You coming too?' asked Russell.

'Part of the way.'

'What's your name?' asked Russell, thinking he could at least get another word out of him.

'Wally,' he replied, looking at Russell as they walked down toward the creekbed. 'What's yours?'

'Russell.'

'Good name too,' said Wally, nodding and looking up along the ridgeline.

They walked as quickly as Russell could manage. Despite his quiet friend's assurance, he was still worried about Siao Lin and wanted to reach her as quickly as possible. The day was bright and crisp. If Russell was cold when he started, fifteen minutes of walking had him sweating heavily enough to remove his jacket, and jam it into his backpack.

Half an hour into the walk, Wally turned off and headed up a creekbed which joined from the left. Russell didn't query his departure, just stopped for a few seconds and watched the man's back as he strode away. His loose ragged jeans, with rope for a belt, flopped about, belying his economical gait across the loose shingle. Russell turned his head and looked downstream, then recommenced slogging along in the soft, sandy, gravelly streambed.

The sun was almost overhead by the time he trudged up the last slope and crested a slight ridge to gain a view down to the hotsprings. Siao Lin was there, sitting near what Russell first thought was a dead body. It turned out to be a body, only it wasn't quite dead. Siao Lin looked up when she heard his footsteps. She stood and walked to him. They hugged each other, both looking relieved.

'What happened?' asked Russell.

'He was too good for me not to hurt him seriously,' Siao Lin was crying. Russell could see from her red eyes she'd been at it a while too.

'Why did he decide to fight you?'

She told Russell how Ming Sen had sent the other men off to chase two aborigines. He'd already implied she was going to be killed, so she took a chance and kicked the gun from his hands. Maybe she'd challenged his honour in doing so, or perhaps he'd never really taken her as a serious threat. Whatever the reason, Ming Sen had told her he didn't need the gun and come straight at her. Siao Lin said she realised very quickly the fight had to be ended hastily, she was too weak to do anything else.

'You were only defending yourself Siao Lin,' said Russell, in an effort to soothe her.

'No,' she admitted, shaking her head. 'At the end I had to finish it. I used a killing move, he had no chance. I think he thought he could always fall back on his gun.'

Russell hugged her again and then called Dave, in Adelaide. He asked for a chopper. Dave said he hoped Russell was joking, but seemed to be happy enough once told they had a live Zihnjihn agent. Dave reckoned a couple of hours. Russell told Siao Lin and she appeared to relax a bit. He walked to the hotsprings and stripped to his underwear before easing into the hot waters. Siao Lin asked if he was alright. Russell said he was feeling a few cramps from being tied up day and night. As he soaked, Russel told her about being saved by an aborigine named Wally, who killed the agent guarding him with a boomerang. Siao Lin grinned, laughing in a tense, relieved sort of way before she went on to tell him about Jeffrey and Wally, as she followed Russell's example and slipped into the hot waters.

The chopper arrived three hours later and they loaded Ming Sen aboard. He was conscious but said nothing at all. Russell walked Siao Lin to the door and tried to help her in. She stepped aside.

'I'm not going,' she said, surprising him yet again. 'I'll walk back and get the Landcruiser, the samples we need are in it.'

'We can fly back there in a couple of minutes,' said Russell, thinking he really didn't want to leave her up there alone.

'I'd rather walk a bit,' she said. 'I need to clear my head and I need some space.'

Movement off to my right caught Russell's attention. An aborigine nodded a greeting as he looked at him. They're coming out of the bloody woodwork, he thought, figuring Siao Lin would be alright. He looked at her and nodded before climbing into the chopper.

She told him she'd be out of the mountains within a day or two and would give him a call then. She kept talking; her banter reminding Russell of something he'd have done if he'd been trying to cover up what he was really feeling.

'We've changed each other, haven't we,' said Russell, cutting across her conversation.

'I suppose we have,' she nodded in agreement. 'You should look after Una Russell.

'She can look after herself well enough,' replied Russell quickly. Una's tougher than me, he thought. Whether she was his soft spot or not, he didn't want to talk about her.

'She's not as strong as you tell yourself Russell,' said Siao Lin. 'She acts tougher than she is.'

'What are you gonna' do then?' asked Russell, changing the subject, he knew Siao Lin was right.

'Take what I want,' she said. 'Isn't that what you'd do.'

She stepped forward and kissed him briefly on the lips, then turned and walked quickly away from the chopper. She looked so small and slim, he thought; and frail. How had she taken out a trained agent who'd put him on his back in a second. The pilot reached across and pulled the door shut with a crunch. Once Siao Lin was clear, she turned to face the chopper and lifted her arm in farewell. The pilot started the engine. After the warm up, as the rotors swivelled to lift, clouds of debris spread out and about. The last glimpse Russell had of Siao Lin was her turning to run back toward the hot springs, to escape the swirling cloud of sand and dust.

35 — Que Serah

What the future brought was never something Russell worried about too much. He'd learned to cope with, even to expect, obstacles and assaults. He was well steeled against insult, injury and anything else he could imagine. Perhaps Siao Lin was someone he had never quite been able to come to terms with. As he thought of her he smiled, almost laughing out loud as he realised his image of her was larger than life, like a movie character. Una, on the other hand, also in his thoughts, seemed far more down to earth. Simpler in fact; easier for him to understand, despite her hard shell and easy going bloke-type dialogue. She'd been around.

Russell got on with the follow up duties, he was always glad when paper work was wrapped up. Then he felt he was ready for the next job. Within three days he'd even had all the gold money put into Siao Lin's account. They just needed a few details from her and they could sign off on the whole gold and cobalt business.

For two days he had set up an itinerary for a new job, and then chaperoned the dignitary from a small Pacific nation. And if the assignment was boring, it was safe and relaxed; Bill, his partner for the job was back in good form after having saved the day in the mountains. Late in the afternoon, they dropped the bigwig off at the airport and headed straight for the bar. Russell was happy with the relationship between them, especially so after a few beers. He watched Bill through the faint haze of inebriation. He's not the same though, he thought. Bill caught his gaze.

'I'll tell you this once Russ,' he said, voice faintly slurred. 'I was wrong mate, but you 'aint gonna' get no apology outa' me. Not ever. Okay?'

'Fair enough,' Russell nodded, holding Bills gaze. That's the difference, he thought, suddenly enlightened; we're even now, in the saving each other's life stakes.

When Siao Lin finally phoned him, a week and a half after he'd left her by Paralana Hotsprings, he was simply, pleasantly surprised and happy to hear from her. Firstly, she apologised for not having phoned sooner and then enquired as to how his recovery was going.

Russell let her know all was well, told her how he'd finished another job since, and even been to the gym a couple of times, getting back into shape. As he lied about the gym, he wondered why she was calling, and asked if she'd returned to Adelaide. There was a distinct pause. He asked her where she was and heard laughter, and another voice; speaking Chinese, of course he didn't understand a word of it.

Siao Lin told him she was taking a break up near Coffs Harbour and her friend Mai Ling was with her. She changed the subject by asking how Una was. Russell admitted he hadn't seen her yet, said he hadn't had time, but intended to soon. Siao Lin suggested strongly that he do so right away.

Russell told her she sounded like his Mum, apart from the accent. Changing the subject, he asked her about the rock samples and she laughed. Russell said he didn't think it was a funny question at all, adding that Dave had been on his back for the last bloody week about them. Siao Lin apologised again and said she'd completed the petrological examinations. They matched perfectly with the samples she'd taken from the gold, and she'd both submitted samples to AMDEL for analysis and received the results back.

She said she could email rough details in a few minutes, but had already sent copies of the maps and plans to Una's address. Siao Lin added that she had already cancelled her claim near the Wheal Frost and filed a lease over the small valley where the gold and cobalt were located.

The details shook Russell a bit. Another surprise, but on thinking it over he decided why not. Fair dues to her if she was right on the ball. He knew she'd well over a million and a half dollars from the gold alone, now it looked like she had the lease on an area which lots of big mining companies were trying pretty hard to claim.

Russell took the rest of that day to dry out; he'd been drinking a lot since his return, the last few nights with Bill had been pretty full on. Early the next day he finally called to see Una. Morning was never the best time for him; one coffee just didn't do it. He started to tell Una what had happened, after all, he'd said he would explain what had been going on. It was definitely not stuff he should have talked about at all, but he felt obliged. Within a couple of minutes Una was simply asking questions, which of course Russell answered. Her first question was what had happened between himself and Siao Lin. Russell told her, half expecting a jealous outburst. He was surprised yet again! If it bothered her at all, she kept it bloody well hidden, even had a bit of a chuckle at how they were surprised so easily, twice by two different sets of bad guys.

'Something I do need to tell you,' she admitted.

Russell nodded for her to go ahead.

'Remember Mai Ling?' she asked.

He nodded again, wondering what she was on about.

'It appears Siao Lin and her are an item.'

'Siao Lin and Mai Ling?' asked Russel, at first not being able to assimilate and then to accept what she'd said.

He spent ten wasted minutes trying to explain to her how Siao Lin couldn't be gay. Eventually he gave it up. Siao Lin was gone, but Una was still there, which suited him just fine. They shared a laugh at his expense.

She told him that Siao Lin had already sent a parcel to her. A lot of it was for Russell and the *Organisation*, but it had included a letter thanking Una for her help when Siao Lin had been in Adelaide.

'I can't take it,' said Una as she extracted a bundle of maps and plans from a drawer and handed them to him.

'Can't take what?' He was totally confused.

'I was talking to Siao Lin before the two of you left for the mountains, raving about wanting to buy my own house one day,' Una was wide eyed. 'She sent me a cheque.'

'A cheque?'

'A cheque for $250,000.'

Russell had another bit of a laugh and went on to tell her about the gold her great great grandfather had discovered and that Siao Lin had already cashed in a million and a half.

'So it's real?' she asked.

Russell nodded, this time the laugh was on Una.

'I can't take it though, can I,' she sounded pretty adamant, with just a faint element of doubt in her tone.

'Consider two things,' he said, smiling. 'If Siao Lin sent it, she meant it to be accepted. Second thing, having this place to stay could well have saved her life. There were some pretty bad people hunting for her. Take it and buy a house.'

'Guess you're right,' she said. 'Now that you put it that way, I'll get it into the bank this arvo.'

Russell finished the Javan coffee she'd made, and took a deep breath before standing.

'Come on girl,' he said, extending his hand to her. 'Let's go and take a walk on a beach, get some fresh air. Got a few more things to tell you yet.'

36 — Job Offer

I walked back, a little way beyond the circle of the blades and tried to wave, but the helicopter began to lift and a blinding cloud of dust and flying debris spread out. I couldn't see. It was scary and felt dangerous, so I ran back toward the hotsprings. A little while later, through still watery eyes, I caught the briefest glimpse of the chopper disappearing over the edge of the Freeling heights 600 metres overhead and a kilometre or so to the west.

I stood by the hotsprings awhile, my ears were ringing. I rubbed my eyes to clear some of the dust and thought on what Russell had said; that we'd swapped characters. I could see the change now he'd mentioned it, but wouldn't have noticed it myself, as the alteration had been gradual. It was only a small change anyway. He didn't even realise he was bound to Una yet, but I reckoned she had more of an idea. I liked her, it was easy to see her tough act was covering up her vulnerability and she was a nice person.

The sun overhead reminded me I was still standing beside the hotsprings and I still had a couple of hours of walking to do. The long upstream walk was what I needed, gave me time to think. The air was cool enough when I started out and though I warmed to the walk initially, it was bloody cold for the last third. The sun kept vanishing behind the steep cliffs to the west and north. I thought about lots of things; mainly about the hardly believable events of the last week. I wondered what I really wanted to do next. By the time I arrived, two hours later, I'd decided I was simply going to do what I wanted. What was expected of me would be irrelevant, and anyway, for the present all I wanted was to be warm again.

Once at the campsite, I lit a really big fire and warmed myself well as the evening closed in. It took me until full dark to pack up Russell's tent and all the gear we'd spread about the area. I ate quickly and went to sleep as soon as it was dark, thinking it would be good to rise early.

I woke early enough, but went back to sleep; it was frosty outside. I didn't manage to struggle out of the sleeping bag until the sun had warmed the tent. The morning was glacial, and after a quick breakfast, using up the last food and water, it took a further hour to load the car and I was finally on my way. It felt good to be going somewhere I wanted at last, and though the road to the west was just as bumpy and dusty as I remembered from the previous trip, I didn't care. I didn't stop at Copley, much as I would've enjoyed a shower; I turned south and headed straight for Hawker. I ate the sandwich I bought at the service station there as I pressed on. At least it was warm in the car with the heater on.

I drove through Quorn around 4.30 pm, by-passed Pt. Augusta, and arrived at Pt. Pirie around six pm. Mai Ling was waiting for me. I stowed the Landcruiser in her garage, and had a hot shower. I felt clean and alive again. We took a taxi to a restaurant in an old renovated church. My fresh fish and salad was a pleasant change from the supplies Russell and I had taken into the mountains.

The next day, after Mai Ling went off to work at the hospital, I took a cab into the city centre and visited the ANZ bank. I took out $10,000.00 in cash, enough to tide us over for some time. My account balance had soared yet again. Bill or Russell must have had the gold processed and converted to cash already. I wrote a letter to Una in Adelaide, thanking her for letting her stay there. Once again I thought about Una and decided to do what I felt like. I felt I owed her for allowing me to stay with her in Adelaide, but mainly I liked her and wanted to keep in touch. I wanted to help her and I was certainly in a position to do so. I sent her a cheque to help her buy the house she said she'd always wanted. I figured she'd end up with Russell and he'd look after her, but I'd give them a good start, I could afford it.

I also posted off all the specimens I'd packaged the previous night to AMDEL, asking for analyses in both gold and cobalt for all the samples. My business done, I went back to Mae Ling's house and put my feet up.

When Mae returned that evening, she was grinning.

'I did it,' she said as I threw my arms around her. 'I've got two weeks off, starting tomorrow.'

I phoned the airport right away and booked flights, I was sick of being so cold all the time.

The next day we took a morning flight to Adelaide, a connecting flight to Sydney, and finally a flight up to Coffs Harbour.

We booked in to the same place, the Boambee Bay Resort, in Toormina, which I'd stayed at previously. I called my friend Barry and asked him to come and pick us up the following morning. I arranged to hire his cab for the day, telling him we wanted to look at local properties. We ate at the resort and went to bed early, after I took the delighted Mae Ling for a walk down to the beach. The weather was cool, it was nearly mid-winter, but not nearly as cold as it had been in South Australia.

Luckily for me, Barry knew some people who were selling up and moving further north. After a quick look, I agreed that the house was ideal. In a month I would be able to move in to my own place, 600 metres from the beach and close to shops and schools. The first week slipped by in a blur as I shared my space with Mai Ling. I phoned AMDEL and spoke to Harry Browne; he gave me the sample results and I spent a few days drawing up plans and completing a detailed geological map of the area of the prospect. I named it Tamo's prospect, after my great great grandfather. I bundled up the plans and sent them off to Una's address, with a brief letter, addressed to her and Russell. I also called the Department of Mines to cancel the claim I'd made near the Wheal Frost, and surprisingly, found out that the area where the gold had come from was still free. On the spur of the moment, I decided to register a claim over the small valley myself. Mai Ling applied for and was offered a job at the base hospital in Coffs Harbour.

I rang Russell on his mobile, told him I was in good shape and apologised for not contacting him sooner. I laughed when he showed surprise at where I was, and told him I'd already sent copies of plans and details of Tamo's prospect to Una's. I also told him that he had better call and see her.

After two weeks, Mae flew back to Pt. Pirie to work for three weeks before leaving her job there. She was happy enough to drive up in the Landcruiser, when she travelled back to Coffs Harbour. The very next day, I got a call from Peter Millar, who asked to meet me, saying he'd be in Coffs the following day. I didn't question how he'd found me, but decided I would meet him, and suggested the Coffs Hotel around eight in the evening. I had already decided to give him the benefit of the doubt, Russell thought he was alright, but I was still darn sure I was going to do what I felt like.

Peter firstly apologised for all the confusion he had created by not being more direct. I was quick to agree that there was indeed a lot of confusion but added I understood Exminoil didn't seem to have done anything inimical toward me.

'Not yet you mean,' Peter was grinning.

He still reminded me of a cross between an imp and a small child when he smiled.

'What do you mean?' I asked, confused and probably saying what he wanted me to say.

'Firstly Siao Lin, we'd like to offer you a job as chief geologist,' he was still smiling.

I laughed. Covering up my bewilderment I guess, his remark was totally unexpected.

'Serious,' he said, sounding a bit more serious too. 'We really want you working for us.'

'What did you mean when you said, "Not yet", a few seconds ago?' I asked.

'Remember the contract you signed when you first took the job with us?' he asked.

I nodded. He's really serious I thought.

'I told you when we paid you out that legally, you were still working for us for the following year,' he continued.

'Yes, I remember,' I said, lifting my glass and sipping at the cold juice. 'Go on,' I thought I could see where he was going with this.

Peter was still smiling when he mentioned that as I was still officially employed by Exminoil, I could not take personal advantage of any information gained whilst working for them. He reckoned that meant all the gold and the claim belonged to Exminoil.

I was half a step ahead of him, having already realised what the connotations of his revelation were. I nodded to myself. He was only half right.

'Exminoil can have the claim,' I agreed. 'The gold however, is a quite different matter. It was given to me by my great great grandfather and was not subject to ownership by Exminoil in any way.'

Peter was congenial, agreeing with me, adding that the deposit in the Flinders Ranges was probably too small for them to bother with anyway. He asked how much gold I'd recovered. Surprised me he didn't know.

'But,' he added, after I'd refused to enlighten him. 'When you've had enough of a holiday, you might come back to work for us, we can't easily replace you Siao Lin.'

'I've a few things to do Peter,' I laughed as he took a good slug of his beer. 'You never know though, I might well be looking for a job in a year and a half or so.'

'A year and a half?' asked Peter, obviously flabbergasted.

'I'm pregnant,' I laughed again. Peter didn't see the joke at all. 'Got to have a baby and bring it up for a while first, but then I may well take you up on your offer.'

'I'll drink to that,' said Peter, and he certainly did.

Several weeks later, I sat alone on the beach at the south end of Toormina, watching waves crash across the rocks and reefs of a craggy island. We'd settled into our new house and Mai Ling was working days at the Base hospital. I sat back, warm in the shelter of the dunes at the back of the beach, amazed at how far I'd come. I had a pleasant feeling of freedom and elation. I have followed in the footsteps of my ancestor, even glimpsed him within the personality of the giant of my opium vision. Since then I have asserted myself far beyond what I would have imagined a few months earlier. I know I will be happy to have my child; raising it with my partner Mai Ling will be no effort. I can work a little when I like, if I want, but I've no need to.

A deep rumble of thunder dragged my thoughts back to the windswept beach. I lay back in the warm sand and watched a thunderstorm approaching from the sea. The lightning took me back to a drilling platform off the coast of New Guinea; to the time I was forced to defend myself. I smiled, remembering but no longer worrying at what I had done. The mental ghost of the man I killed has long since ceased to bother me. Time has inserted adequate distance between me and the event. I can't see the future and neither would I want to, I have my memories and more importantly I have discovered the pleasure of the present.

37 — Paralana

They met out the front of the small, ramshackle shop which served the village. The car pulled up near the entrance to the office, a few metres away. The woman was 76, with grey, close cropped hair, and wearing loose, comfortable looking clothes. Her son had remained in the car whilst she got out and walked around to where an old Aborigine stood slowly from the plastic bench by the shop's front door. He looked to be in his eighties, with white hair and beard, and his loose jeans were tied with rope. The two hugged as long lost friends, people who'd shared an adventure a long time ago or could see a future where they would mingle their characters.

'Ah Geoffrey,' she smiled. 'You have even more wrinkles than me.'

They both laughed aloud.

'You must meet my son, Russell,' she laughed and waved to the car.

Her son got out and walked across to them.

'He looks like his dad Siao Lin,' said Geoffrey.

'You still remember what he looked like,' laughed Siao Lin. 'After 50 years have rushed by.'

'I remember,' he smiled at her. 'Ah, but now, closer up, I see he has a little of the oriental flavour too.'

'Can't help where you come from,' said the younger man, joining their conversation, smiling and holding out his hand to Geoffrey. 'Only where you go. I've heard a bit about you.'

Geoffrey shook hands with the younger man and nodded.

'Good handshake,' he said clearly.

'Hot springs or Wheal Frost?' she asked. Geoffrey looked from her son and met her eyes.

'These old bones tell me Paralana,' he said, stretching his arms skyward. A warming sun shone from a hazy sky.

They walked to the car and climbed in. Russell started it, backed out, swung around and headed out the hard packed dirt road to the east. Dust clouds followed them and spread amongst the dry brush crowding against the edge of the road.

The car pulled up at the hotsprings as the last sun shone on the green algal mats floating on the water's surface. The two older people walked to the water and, removing most of their clothes, walked into the pool, sweeping aside the thick layer of algae as wisps of steam swirled about them.

The younger man set up a shelter and laid out two sleeping bags, two chairs, a table, a couple of bottles and an esky of food. He then drove off, leaving the two soaking in the hot waters.

In the morning, young Russell returned and packed up the equipment. Siao Lin and Geoffrey stepped out of the hot water and began to dry themselves.

'I am surprised we didn't dream the giant last night,' said Siao Lin with a sudden brightness to her eye.

'The giant,' Geoffrey laughed. 'I saw him. You should be thankful for a few more years of life girl.'

'You'll be staying then?' asked Siao Lin as she opened the car door and noticed Geoffrey hanging back.

Geoffrey nodded. She walked to him and hugged him for a few seconds, then held him at arm's length, peering through her thick glasses.

'I am thankful Geoffrey,' she said seriously. 'Thankful for my life and all the help you gave me. Until we meet again.'

The two of them laughed. Siao Lin walked back to the car and climbed in beside her son. The car drove off, trailing red dust.

Siao Lin dozed for a lot of the trip southward, the late lunch in Burra was pleasant enough. If her son was tired by the drive, he didn't show it, nor say anything much. She was happy enough not to speak, feeling both happy at meeting Geoffrey after so long and sad she wouldn't meet him again in her life. What happened when she died wasn't something she worried about at all. She knew the dreamtime wasn't forever, but it was certainly longer than she could imagine, and it certainly wasn't measured in years.

As they drove through bustling, evening traffic on the outskirts of Adelaide, she asked her son to drop her by the lake, before he dropped off the hire car at the airport. She said she'd get a taxi out later, their flight wasn't until nine.

The Lake of the Torrens River was a quite different place; the seat where she'd first met Russell had been replaced with a new, multi-coloured plastic one. She walked through the busy streets, along the mall, choked with chattering shoppers and numerous street vendors. Walking out of the clutter and bustle, Siao Lin found herself in the same park she had visited as a young woman. To her surprise she discovered, as she'd actually half expected, that an old man was sitting on the grass, playing a guitar. There were no aborigines visible and the bushes where they had grouped had been replaced with the humpy concrete of a deserted skate track. She sat on a nearby bench and listened as the man began to sing:

> 'Some songs I sing
> are never written down,
> very rarely played at all
> to other ears.
> The wind is high,
> come fill your wings,
> I'd touch the sky,
> if I could hear you sing…'

She shut her eyes to concentrate on the song; the guitar and words were tranquil and mesmerising. The song felt sad, but felt herself smile, she knew it was real. Almost right away she saw her beloved mountains, clear as day. A view from above, far above; not from an aeroplane, but through the eyes of the giant. She could feel the giant smiling as he listened to the song.

> 'They say no man's an island,
> but look at all this sea,
> look at all these waves,
> between yourself and me…'

'Those words suit perfectly,' it was Geoffrey's voice. A tear flushed from a closed eye.

'Fare well Geoffrey, she said.' She was also aware of Tamo, he suddenly waxed strongly within the amalgamation of entities who shaped the giant.

'You only sense me more strongly because we have a blood connection,' he said. She could hear the relaxed smile within his tone. 'It is good to know you Siao Lin.'

She sensed Russell for a moment too, he felt far, far away, and was soon gone. She watched the mountains below and listened to the song too.

> 'Are you coming back again
> for just a little while,
> doesn't matter anyway
> I've learned to smile...'

Am I asleep again, she thought. Yet as she opened her eyes, a clear view of two gnarled and ancient river red gums crystalised in her vision. Between them stood the same youth with the big grin.

'You haven't aged at all,' she said, recognizing him easily.

'You nearly finished down there now girly,' he laughed. 'Anyway, I'm really very very old.'

Siao Lin found herself laughing too. She knew what he meant and accepted it. She kept on smiling, even when she opened her eyes to a cold Adelaide day, with soft rain spitting from a featureless grey sky.

> 'Some songs I sing
> are never written down,
> very rarely played at all
> to other ears.'

The song finished. Realising he must be the older version of the youth who had played songs, helped her with visions in her younger days, Siao Lin called for the old man to sit with her. He obliged with a smile, and she asked him about himself. He told her a tale of living in Ireland for twenty years, playing music for a living. He was retired and living in northern NSW, and had returned to Adelaide to attend the funeral of his father.

She had half expected him to have knowledge of what had

occurred to her and yet was somehow relieved he didn't seem to. It was a strange coincidence that he actually lived quite close to where she did, near Coffs harbour. It is a coincidence isn't it, she thought?

He told her he thought he remembered one of the times she'd listened to him play. Later that day he'd watched a one armed aboriginal man play the guitar and sing, not something which could easily be forgotten.

'You gave them some money,' she said, remembering. 'That was the day I first met Geoffrey.'

'I always gave them money,' he said, smiling at the memories, nodding faintly as he recalled. 'I spoke to Geoffrey many years ago, but I knew Wally better.'

Ten minutes later, still smiling, Siao Lin hailed a taxi to the airport. They'd be back in Coffs Harbour the following day. Adelaide in winter was too cold for old bones, be good to see Mai Ling and her grandchildren again. She hadn't been gone long, but it seemed to be ages. Why did time go by in such a hurry? But then it didn't matter did it. It didn't matter at all.

That evening, Siao Lin arrived in the airport at Coffs and was met by Barry's son, Martin, also a cabby, like his father had been.

'You go ahead Russell,' she said when they arrived outside.

She spoke to Martin for a while, asking after Barry and the rest of the family. As she walked to the front door and opened it, she was at first confused by two strangers waiting inside, grinning at her. Then she spotted Mai, standing behind them smiling, and at once realized who they were. Russell and Una. She'd thought they were in Ireland.

'Finally managed to give you a surprise,' said Russell, his voice as deep as ever.

'You did that,' she agreed, stepping forward. The three of them embraced with a warmth made awkward with age.

'Good to see you again Siao Lin,' said Una as they separated. 'We came over to Aus' to see our kids and grandkids, thought we'd call in and say hi.'

She felt Mai touch her hand and was just happy to be home. They all walked to the lounge room.

'Have you seen that Giant lately?' asked Russell softly as he walked close beside her.

'I have indeed,' she smiled at his question.

'He reckons he's my Dad,' her son Russell interrupted her train of thought, pointing at Russell, then stepped forward and hugged her.

'How else would you get such an ugly mug,' laughed Siao Lin returning his hug.

www.ingramcontent.com/pod-product-compliance
Lightning Source LLC
Chambersburg PA
CBHW030301130626
46549CB00002B/643